"UP AND DOWN THE WORLD I HAVE WANDERED, LEAVING HORROR AND SLAUGHTER IN MY TRAIL...

"No one knows of my frightful double life, since no one could recognize me in the clutch of the demon; and few, seeing me, live to tell of it.

"My hands are red, my soul doomed to everlasting flames, my mind is torn with remorse for my crimes. And yet I can do nothing to help myself.... You see before you a man fiend-haunted for all eternity."

The moon rose and peered in at the barred windows.... And then the hand of horror grasped me. On the wall behind him appeared a shadow, a shadow clearly defined of a wolf's head!

WOLFSHEAD

From the pen of the master of horror
Robert E. Howard
Creator of Conan

Bantam Science Fiction and Fantasy
Ask your bookseller for the books you have missed

CONAN THE SWORDSMAN by L. Sprague de Camp, Lin Carter and Bjorn Nyberg
CONAN THE LIBERATOR by L. Sprague de Camp and Lin Carter
KULL by Robert E. Howard
SOLOMON KANE: SKULLS IN THE STARS by Robert E. Howard
SOLOMON KANE: THE HILLS OF THE DEAD by Robert E. Howard
THE SWORD OF SKELOS by Andrew Offutt
WOLFSHEAD by Robert E. Howard

WOLFSHEAD

Robert E. Howard

WOLFSHEAD
A Bantam Book / September 1979

ACKNOWLEDGMENTS

"The Black Stone," *Copyright 1931 by Popular Fiction Publishing Company for* Weird Tales, *November 1931.*

"The Valley of the Worm," *Copyright 1934 by Popular Fiction Publishing Company for* Weird Tales, *February 1934.*

"Wolfshead," *Copyright 1926 by Popular Fiction Publishing Company for* Weird Tales, *April 1926.*

"The Fire of Asshurbanipal," *Copyright 1936 by Popular Fiction Publishing Company for* Weird Tales, *December 1936.*

"The House of Arabu," *Copyright 1951 by Avon Novels Inc. (under the title* "The Witch from Hell's Kitchen,"*) for* Avon Fantasy Reader *No. 18.*

"The Horror from the Mound," *Copyright 1932 by Popular Fiction Publishing Company for* Weird Tales, *May 1932.*

All rights reserved.
Copyright © 1979 by Alla Ray Kuykendall
and Alla Ray Morris.
Cover art copyright © 1979 by Bantam Books, Inc.
This book may not be reproduced in whole or in part, by mimeograph or any other means, without permission.
For information address: Bantam Books, Inc.

ISBN 0-533-12353-X

Published simultaneously in the United States and Canada

Bantam Books are published by Bantam Books, Inc. Its trademark, consisting of the words "Bantam Books" and the portrayal of a bantam, is Registered in U.S. Patent and Trademark Office and in other countries. Marca Registrada. Bantam Books, Inc., 666 Fifth Avenue, New York, New York 10019

PRINTED IN THE UNITED STATES OF AMERICA

Contents

Introduction by Robert Bloch	1
The Black Stone	5
The Valley of the Worm	25
Wolfshead	49
The Fire of Asshurbanipal	75
The House of Arabu	102
The Horror from the Mound	128

WOLFSHEAD

Introduction

That sound you hear is probably Kirk Mashburn turning over in his grave.

I assume, of course, that he is dead. Well over forty years have passed since Mr. Mashburn, a distinguished contributor to *Weird Tales* magazine, wrote to the letter column and denounced me for criticizing the work of fellow-author Robert E. Howard.

And here I am today, writing an introduction to a volume of Howard's stories.

Actually it's not all that strange. I could easily have written such an introduction even then. For my youthfully intemperate remarks were directed at Howard's Conan series which I deemed inferior to his other work. It was my feeling that his talent was best employed in tales such as "The Valley of the Worm" and similar material represented in this present volume.

But loyal Conan fans chose to equate intemperance with blasphemy. As I recall, Mr. Mashburn made tactfully restrained references to "polecat ethics"—and a gentleman calling himself Fred Anger offered an equally mature response. He was, he said, "petrified with anguish and horror" upon learning that my own initially published story had tied for first place in the readers' affections. His psychological insight was that this "only goes to prove that old adage that some people are born crazy and others get that way."

Introduction

At the tender age of seventeen I was somewhat startled by what I even then felt to be a tempest in a chamberpot. The pole-categorization by a respectable Southern author and gentleman bewildered me. And the attacks of the aptly named Mr. Anger, which continued for several years, seemed a form of overkill.

Today I can look back upon the episode with a more charitable eye. Whatever that eye didn't perceive in Howard's Conan saga has been amply recognized by others. Conan has survived through the years as sturdily as he did in the stories, and fittingly champions Howard's fame.

So it is that I can no longer take issue with the proven merits of this character, and I have long forgiven those who questioned my temerity. If Mr. Mashburn has, as I suspect, gone to his final reward, I pray this introduction will not disturb his rest. As for Mr. Anger, who has also vanished from my ken, I wish him only the best. I hope he is alive and well and happily wed to a typical Conan-story heroine—though at one time I admit I would like to have seen him married to Wilbur Whateley's mother.

We come now to the work of Robert E. Howard represented in this volume. Some of us have come to these stories before, and over the years we frequently returned to find renewed enjoyment in his picaresque portrayals and the imaginative settings he created.

For others, this may be their first venture into Howard's colorful domain. It is to them that I address myself here—and to those whose reading has been limited to the Conan series.

In order to fully appreciate the tales that follow, it is necessary to consider the milieu in which they originated.

First of all, one must bear in mind Robert E. Howard's personal background. He was a country doctor's son, born and bred in a rough, raw region of what had recently been the Wild West and living out the last years of his brief life in a tiny Texas town. Howard was big

Introduction

and burly, handy with his fists, and like many of his fellow citizens he frequently toted a pistol.

But there the resemblance ended. For Robert E. Howard was a lifelong reader, a writer from early adolescence on. And behind the facade of machismo he led the secret life of a dreamer and a poet.

Dreamers and poets were not comfortable figures in that time and place. And even when Howard began to earn a respectable income from published writing, he received less than his just due from local friends and neighbors. As a result he concealed his inner imperatives; he strove to emphasize the image of a "typical" Westerner and even went so far as to caricature himself in the genre-stories he wrote dealing with that region.

Those privileged to know Howard intimately attest that he was by nature a simple and direct man, with humorous awareness regarding the crudities and stupidities of his unimaginative peer group. But it must have been a continuing ordeal for him to maintain his macho masquerade and pretend to suffer fools gladly.

Inevitably this took its toll. There were physical fugues consisting of long, frantic drives across the endless prairies—and mental fugues of even greater consequence, taking the form of delusions of persecution. Howard came to believe that he had mortal enemies—and in the end, when his beloved mother died, he took his own life. He was just thirty years old.

It was, of course, a tragic conclusion to a career which seemed on the point of soaring. Ironically, it now appears that the enemies were merely the product of his imagination. Whereas actually Robert E. Howard had thousands of friends—the army of devoted readers who enjoyed the tales which were also the product of his imagination.

This imagination frequently turned towards the world of the past. Not the known world, but a terra incognita of his own creation—a realm peopled by primitive man or his direct descendants; barbarian

Introduction

warriors, wizards and worshippers of dark gods in the forgotten civilizations of lands long lost. Some of these characters were frankly racists by today's standards, but Howard was not painting a picture of today. His world sprawled over a broad canvas and its *chiaroscuro* served to highlight heroic figures larger than life. But though deceptively drawn in black-and-white, certain nuances are immediately visible. Howard's heroes may believe in direct action, yet they are brooders at the prey of emotional forces they cannot control. Frequently they are governed by obscure premonition and instinctual reaction; often they go berserk. They loathe reptiles, mistrust the stunted and the deformed, fear the unknown even as they bravely face it.

Today's intelligentsia may find it easy to dismiss such responses with a sneer, but I venture to say that the late Carl Jung would recognize them. Howard's archetypal characters, his emphasis on atavism and racial memories, are closely allied to Jung's theories of psychology, and he would observe them with understanding.

And those who—like Howard himself—yearn for far-off and fanciful kingdoms of high adventure, of daring deeds and daring men who counter cunning with courage and conquer evil at whatever cost, will not only understand but enjoy these tales.

There are stories in modern settings amongst those which follow here, but the basic pattern of attitudes prevails. And if one bears in mind that modernity is a relative term, then the stylistic excesses common to these sagas written forty-odd years ago can be easily excused. For behind them lurks a dark poetry, and the timeless truth of dreams.

That is why these tales have survived. They remain a fitting heritage of the poet and dreamer who was Robert E. Howard.

—ROBERT BLOCH

The Black Stone

*They say foul things of Old Times still lurk
In dark forgotten corners of the world,
And Gates still gape to loose, on certain nights,
Shapes pent in Hell.*
—JUSTIN GEOFFREY

I read of it first in the strange book of Von Junzt, the German eccentric who lived so curiously and died in such grisly and mysterious fashion. It was my fortune to have access to his Nameless Cults in the original edition, the so-called Black Book, published in Düsseldorf in 1839, shortly before a hounding doom overtook the author. Collectors of rare literature were familiar with Nameless Cults mainly through the cheap and faulty translation which was pirated in London by Bridewall in 1845, and the carefully expurgated edition put out by the Golden Goblin Press of New York, 1909. But the volume I stumbled upon was one of the unexpurgated German copies, with heavy black leather covers and rusty iron hasps. I doubt if there are more than half a dozen such volumes in the entire world today, for the quantity issued was not great, and when the manner of the author's demise was bruited about, many possessors of the book burned their volumes in panic.

The Black Stone

Von Junzt spent his entire life (1795-1840) delving into forbidden subjects; he traveled in all parts of the world, gained entrance into innumerable secret societies, and read countless little-known and esoteric books and manuscripts in the original; and in the chapters of the Black Book, which range from startling clarity of exposition to murky ambiguity, there are statements and hints to freeze the blood of a thinking man. Reading what Von Junzt dared put in print arouses uneasy speculations as to what it was that he dared not tell. What dark matters, for instance, were contained in those closely written pages that formed the unpublished manuscript on which he worked unceasingly for months before his death, and which lay torn and scattered all over the floor of the locked and bolted chamber in which Von Junzt was found dead with the marks of taloned fingers on his throat? It will never be known, for the author's closest friend, the Frenchman Alexis Ladeau, after having spent a whole night piecing the fragments together and reading what was written, burnt them to ashes and cut his own throat with a razor.

But the contents of the published matter are shuddersome enough, even if one accepts the general view that they but represent the ravings of a madman. There among many strange things I found mention of the Black Stone, that curious, sinister monolith that broods among the mountains of Hungary, and about which so many dark legends cluster. Van Junzt did not devote much space to it—the bulk of his grim work concerns cults and objects of dark worship which he maintained existed in his day, and it would seem that the Black Stone represents some order or being lost and forgotten centuries ago. But he spoke of it as one of the keys—a phrase used many times by him, in various relations, and constituting one of the obscurities of his work. And he hinted briefly at curious sights to be seen about the monolith on Midsummer Night. He mentioned Otto Dostmann's theory that this monolith was a remnant of the Hunnish

The Black Stone

invasion and had been erected to commemorate a victory of Attila over the Goths. Von Junzt contradicted this assertion without giving any refutory facts, merely remarking that to attribute the origin of the Black Stone to the Huns was as logical as assuming that William the Conqueror reared Stonehenge.

This implication of enormous antiquity piqued my interest immensely and after some difficulty I succeeded in locating a rat-eaten and moldering copy of Dostmann's Remnants of Lost Empires (Berlin, 1809, "Der Drachenhaus" Press). I was disappointed to find that Dostmann referred to the Black Stone even more briefly than had Von Junzt, dismissing it with a few lines as an artifact comparatively modern in contrast with the Greco-Roman ruins of Asia Minor which were his pet theme. He admitted his inability to make out the defaced characters on the monolith but pronounced them unmistakably Mongoloid. However, little as I learned from Dostmann, he did mention the name of the village adjacent to the Black Stone—Stregoicavar—an ominous name, meaning something like Witch-Town.

A close scrutiny of guidebooks and travel articles gave me no further information—Stregoicavar, not on any map that I could find, lay in a wild, little-frequented region, out of the path of casual tourists. But I did find subject for thought in Dornly's Magyar Folklore. In his chapter on Dream Myths he mentions the Black Stone and tells of some curious superstitions regarding it—especially the belief that if anyone sleeps in the vicinity of the monolith, that person will be haunted by monstrous nightmares for ever after; and he cited tales of the peasants regarding too-curious people who ventured to visit the Stone on Midsummer Night and who died raving mad because of something they saw there.

That was all I could gleam from Dornly, but my interest was even more intensely roused as I sensed a distinctly sinister aura about the Stone. The suggestion of dark antiquity, the recurrent hint of unnatural events on

The Black Stone

Midsummer Night, touched some slumbering instinct in my being, as one senses, rather than hears, the flowing of some dark subterranean river in the night.

And I suddenly saw a connection between this Stone and a certain weird and fantastic poem written by the mad poet, Justin Geoffrey: The People of the Monolith. Inquiries led to the information that Geoffrey had indeed written that poem while traveling in Hungary, and I could not doubt that the Black Stone was the very monolith to which he referred in his strange verse. Reading his stanzas again, I felt once more the strange dim stirrings of subconscious promptings that I had noticed when first reading of the Stone.

I had been casting about for a place to spend a short vacation and I made up my mind. I went to Stregoicavar. A train of obsolete style carried me from Temesvar to within striking distance, at least, of my objective, and a three days' ride in a jouncing coach brought me to the little village which lay in a fertile valley high up in the fir-clad mountains.

The journey itself was uneventful, but during the first day we passed the old battlefield of Schomvaal where the brave Polish-Hungarian knight, Count Boris Vladinoff, made his gallant and futile stand against the victorious hosts of Suleiman the Magnificent, when the Grand Turk swept over eastern Europe in 1526.

The driver of the coach pointed out to me a great heap of crumbling stones on a hill nearby, under which, he said, the bones of the brave Count lay. I remembered a passage from Larson's Turkish Wars. "After the skirmish" (in which the Count with his small army had beaten back the Turkish advance-guard) "the Count was standing beneath the half-ruined walls of the old castle on the hill, giving orders as to the disposition of his forces, when an aide brought to him a small lacquered case which had been taken from the body of the famous Turkish scribe and historian, Selim Bahadur, who had fallen in the fight. The Count took therefrom a roll of parchment and began to read, but he had not read far before he turned

The Black Stone

very pale and, without saying a word, replaced the parchment in the case and thrust the case into his cloak. At that very instant a hidden Turkish battery suddenly opened fire, and the balls striking the old castle, the Hungarians were horrified to see the walls crash down in ruin, completely covering the brave Count. Without a leader the gallant little army was cut to pieces, and in the war-swept years which followed, the bones of the noblemen were never recovered. Today the natives point out a huge and moldering pile of ruins near Schomvaal beneath which, they say, still rests all that the centuries have left of Count Boris Vladinoff."

I found the village of Stregoicavar a dreamy, drowsy little village that apparently belied its sinister cognomen—a forgotten back-eddy that Progress had passed by. The quaint houses and the quainter dress and manners of the people were those of an earlier century. They were friendly, mildly curious but not inquisitive, though visitors from the outside world were extremely rare.

"Ten years ago another American came here and stayed a few days in the village," said the owner of the tavern where I had put up, "a young fellow and queer-acting—mumbled to himself—a poet, I think."

I knew he must mean Justin Geoffrey.

"Yes, he was a poet," I answered, "and he wrote a poem about a bit of scenery near this very village."

"Indeed?" Mine host's interest was aroused. "Then, since all great poets are strange in their speech and actions, he must have achieved great fame, for his actions and conversations were the strangest of any man I ever knew."

"As is usual with artists," I answered, "most of his recognition has come since his death."

"He is dead, then?"

"He died screaming in a madhouse five years ago."

"Too bad, too bad," sighed mine host sympathetically. "Poor lad—he looked too long at the Black Stone."

My heart gave a leap, but I masked my keen interest

The Black Stone

and said casually. "I have heard something of this Black Stone; somewhere near this village, is it not?"

"Nearer than Christian folk wish," he responded. "Look!" He drew me to a latticed window and pointed up at the fir-clad slopes of the brooding blue mountains. "There beyond where you see the bare face of that jutting cliff stands that accursed Stone. Would that it were ground to powder and the powder flung into the Danube to be carried to the deepest ocean! Once men tried to destroy the thing, but each man who laid hammer or maul against it came to an evil end.

"So now the people shun it."

"What is there so evil about it?" I asked curiously.

"It is a demon-haunted thing," he answered uneasily and with the suggestion of a shudder. "In my childhood I knew a young man who came up from below and laughed at our traditions—in his foolhardiness he went to the Stone on Midsummer Night and at dawn stumbled into the village again, stricken dumb and mad. Something had shattered his brain and sealed his lips, for until the day of his death, which came soon after, he spoke only to utter terrible blasphemies or to slaver gibberish.

"My own nephew when very small was lost in the mountains and slept in the woods near the Stone, and now in his manhood he is tortured by foul dreams so that at times he makes the night hideous with his screams and wakes with cold sweat upon him.

"But let us talk of something else, Herr; it is not good to dwell upon such things."

I remarked on the evident age of the tavern and he answered with pride. "The foundations are more than four hundred years old; the original house was the only one in the village which was not burned to the ground when Suleiman's devil swept through the mountains. Here, in the house that then stood on these same foundations, it is said, the scribe Selim Bahadur had his headquarters while ravaging the country hereabouts."

I learned then that the present inhabitants of

The Black Stone

Stregoicavar are not descendants of the people who dwelt there before the Turkish raid of 1526. The victorious Moslems left no living human in the village or the vicinity thereabouts when they passed over. Men, women and children they wiped out in one red holocaust of murder, leaving a vast stretch of country silent and utterly deserted. The present people of Stregoicavar are descended from hardy settlers from the lower valleys who came into the ruined village after the Turk was thrust back.

Mine host did not speak of the extermination of the original inhabitants with any great resentment and I learned that his ancestors in the lower levels had looked on the mountaineers with even more hatred and aversion than they regarded the Turks. He was rather vague regarding the causes of this feud, but said that the original inhabitants of Stregoicavar had been in the habit of making stealthy raids on the lowlands and stealing girls and children. Moreover, he said that they were not exactly of the same blood as his own people; the sturdy, original Magyar-Slavic stock had mixed and intermarried with a degraded aboriginal race until the breeds had blended; producing an unsavory amalgamation. Who these aborigines were, he had not the slightest idea, but maintained that they were "pagans" and had dwelt in the mountains since time immemorial, before the coming of the conquering peoples.

I attached little importance to this tale; seeing in it merely a parallel to the amalgamation of Celtic tribes with Mediterranean aborigines in the Galloway hills, with the resultant mixed race which, as Picts, has such an extensive part in Scotch legendary. Time has a curious foreshortening effect on folklore, and just as tales of the Picts became interwined with legends of an older Mongoloid race, so that eventually the Picts were ascribed the repulsive appearance of the squat primitives, whose individuality merged, in the telling, into Pictish tales, and was forgotten; so, I felt, the supposed inhuman attributes of the first villages of Stregoicavar could be

The Black Stone

traced to older, outworn myths with invading Huns and Mongols.

The morning after my arrival I received directions from mine host, who gave them worriedly, and set out to find the Black Stone. A few hours' tramp up the fir-covered slopes brought me to the face of the rugged, solid stone cliff which jutted boldly from the mountainside. A narrow trail wound up it, and mounting this, I looked out over the peaceful valley of Stregoicavar, which seemed to drowse, guarded on either hand by the great blue mountains. No huts or any sign of human tenancy showed between the cliff whereon I stood and the village. I saw numbers of scattering farms in the valley but all lay on the other side of Stregoicavar, which itself seemed to shrink from the brooding slopes which masked the Black Stone.

The summit of the cliffs proved to be a sort of thickly wooded plateau. I made my way through the dense growth for a short distance and came into a wide glade; and in the center of the glade reared a gaunt figure of black stone.

It was octagonal in shape, some sixteen feet in height and about a foot and a half thick. It had once evidently been highly polished, but now the surface was thickly dinted as if savage efforts had been made to demolish it; but the hammers had done little more than to flake off small bits of stone and mutilate the characters which once had evidently marched up in a spiralling line round and round the shaft to the top. Up to ten feet from the base these characters were almost completely blotted out, so that it was very difficult to trace their direction. Higher up they were plainer, and I managed to squirm part of the way up the shaft and scan them at close range. All were more or less defaced, but I was positive that they symbolized no language now remembered on the face of the earth. I am fairly familiar with all hieroglyphics known to researchers and philologists and I can say, with certainty, that those characters were like nothing of which

The Black Stone

I have ever read or heard. The nearest approach to them that I ever saw were some crude scratches on a gigantic and strangely symmetrical rock in a lost valley of Yucatan. I remember that when I pointed out these marks to the archeologist who was my companion, he maintained that they either represented natural weathering or the idle scratching of some Indian. To my theory that the rock was really the base of a long-vanished column, he merely laughed, calling my attention to the dimensions of it, which suggested, if it were built with any natural rules of architectural symmetry, a column a thousand feet high. But I was not convinced.

I will not say that the characters on the Black Stone were similar to those on that colossal rock in Yucatan; but one suggested the other. As to the substance of the monolith, again I was baffled. The stone of which it was composed was a dully gleaming black, whose surface, where it was not dinted and roughened, created a curious illusion of semi-transparency.

I spent most of the morning there and came away baffled. No connection of the Stone with any other artifact in the world suggested itself to me. It was as if the monolith had been reared by alien hands, in an age distant and apart from human ken.

I returned to the village with my interest in no way abated. Now that I had seen the curious thing, my desire was still more keenly whetted to investigate the matter further and seek to learn by what strange hands and for what strange purpose the Black Stone had been reared in the long ago.

I sought out the tavernkeeper's nephew and questioned him in regard to his dreams, but he was vague, though willing to oblige. He did not mind discussing them, but was unable to describe them with any clarity. Though he dreamed the same dreams repeatedly, and though they were hideously vivid at the time, they left no distinct impression on his waking mind. He remembered them only as chaotic nightmares through which huge whirling fires shot lurid tongues of flames and a black

The Black Stone

drum bellowed incessantly. One thing only he had seen the Black Stone, not on a mountain slope but set like a spire on a colossal black castle.

As for the rest of the villagers I found them not inclined to talk about the Stone, with the exception of the schoolmaster, a man of surprising education, who spent much more of his time out in the world than any of the rest.

He was much interested in what I told him of Von Junzt's remarks about the Stone, and warmly agreed with the German author in the alleged age of the monolith. He believed that a coven had once existed in the vicinity and that possibly all of the original villagers had been members of that fertility cult which once threatened to undermine European civilization and gave rise to the tales of witchcraft. He cited the very name of the village to prove his point; it had not been originally named Stregoicavar, he said; according to legends the builders had called it Xuthltan, which was the aboriginal name of the site on which the village had been built many centuries ago.

This fact roused again an indescribable feeling of uneasiness. The barbarous name did not suggest connection with any Scythic, Slavic or Mongolian race to which an aboriginal people of these mountains would, under natural circumstances, have belonged.

That the Magyars and Slavs of the lower valleys believed the original inhabitants of the village to be members of the witchcraft cult was evident, the schoolmaster said, by the name they gave it, which name continued to be used even after the older settlers had been massacred by the Turks, and the village rebuilt by a cleaner and more wholesome breed.

He did not believe that the members of the cult erected the monolith but he did believe that they used it as a center of the their activities, and repeating vague legends which had been handed down since before the Turkish invasion, he advanced the theory that the degenerate villagers had used it as a sort of altar on which they

The Black Stone

offered human sacrifices, using as victims the girls and babies stolen from his own ancestors in the lower valleys.

He discounted the myths of weird events on Midsummer Night, as well as a curious legend of a strange deity which the witch-people of Xuthltan were said to have invoked with chants and wild rituals of flagellation and slaughter.

He had never visited the Stone on Midsummer Night, he said, but he would not fear to do so; whatever had existed or taken place there in the past, had been long engulfed in the mists of time and oblivion. The Black Stone had lost its meaning save as a link to a dead and dusty past.

It was while returning from a visit with this schoolmaster one night about a week after my arrival at Stregoicavar that a sudden recollection struck me—it was Midsummer Night! The very time that the legends linked with grisly implications to the Black Stone. I turned away from the tavern and strode swiftly through the village. Stregoicavar lay silent; the villagers retired early. I saw no one as I passed rapidly out of the village and up into the firs which masked the mountain's slopes with whispering darkness. A broad silver moon hung above the valley, flooding the crags and slopes in a weird light and etching the shadows blackly. No wind blew through the firs, but a mysterious, intangible rustling and whispering was abroad. Surely on such nights in past centuries, my whimsical imagination told me, naked witches on magic broomsticks had flown across the valley, pursued by jeering demoniac familiars.

I came to the cliffs and was somewhat disquieted to note that the illusive moonlight lent them a subtle appearance I had not noticed before—in the weird light they appeared less like natural cliffs and more like the ruins of cyclopean and Titan-reared battlements jutting from the mountain-slope.

Shaking off this hallucination with difficulty I came upon the plateau and hesitated a moment before I plunged into the brooding darkness of the woods. A sort

The Black Stone

of breathless tenseness hung over the shadows, like an unseen monster holding its breath lest it scare away its prey.

I shook off the sensation a natural one, considering the eeriness of the place and its evil reputation and made my way through the wood, experiencing a most unpleasant sensation that I was being followed, and halting once, sure that something clammy and unstable had brushed against my face in the darkness.

I came out into the glade and saw the tall monolith rearing its gaunt height above the sward. At the edge of the woods on the side toward the cliffs was a stone which formed a sort of natural seat. I sat down, reflecting that it was probably while there that the mad poet, Justin Geoffrey, had written his fantastic People of the Monolith. Mine host thought that it was the Stone which had caused Geoffrey's insanity, but the seeds of madness had been sown in the poet's brain long before he ever came to Stregoicavar.

A glance at my watch showed that the hour of midnight was close at hand. I leaned back, waiting whatever ghostly demonstration might appear. A thin night wind started up among the branches of the firs, with an uncanny suggestion of faint, unseen pipes whispering an eerie and evil tune. The monotony of the sound and my steady gazing at the monolith produced a sort of self-hypnosis upon me; I grew drowsy. I fought this feeling, but sleep stole on me in spite of myself; the monolith seemed to sway and dance, strangely distorted to my gaze, and then I slept.

I opened my eyes and sought to rise, but lay still, as if an icy hand gripped me helpless. Cold terror stole over me. The glade was no longer deserted. It was thronged by a silent crowd of strange people, and my distended eyes took in strange barbaric details of costume which my reason told me were archaic and forgotten even in this backward land. Surely, I thought, these are villagers who have come here to hold some fantastic conclave—but

The Black Stone

another glance told me that these people were not the folk of Stregoicavar. They were a shorter, more squat race, whose brows were lower, whose faces were broader and duller. Some had Slavic and Magyar features, but those features were degraded as from a mixture of some baser, alien strain I could not classify. Many wore the hides of wild beasts, and their whole appearance, both men and women, was one of sensual brutishness. They terrified and repelled me, but they gave me no heed. They formed in a vast half-circle in front of the monolith and began a sort of chant, flinging their arms in unison and weaving their bodies rhythmically from the waist upward. All eyes were fixed on the top of the Stone which they seemed to be invoking. But the strangest of all was the dimness of their voices; not fifty yards from me hundreds of men and women were unmistakably lifting their voices in a wild chant, yet those voices came to me as a faint indistinguishable murmur as if from across vast leagues of Space or time.

Before the monolith stood a sort of brazier from which a vile, nauseous yellow smoke billowed upward, curling curiously in a swaying spiral around the black shaft, like a vast unstable snake.

On one side of this brazier lay two figures a young girl, stark naked and bound hand and foot, and an infant, apparently only a few months old. On the other side of the brazier squatted a hideous old hag with a queer sort of black drum on her lap; this drum she beat with slow, light blows of her open palms, but I could not hear the sound.

The rhythm of the swaying bodies grew faster and into the space between the people and the monolith sprang a naked young woman, her eyes blazing, her long black hair flying loose. Spinning dizzily on her toes, she whirled across the open space and fell prostrate before the Stone, where she lay motionless. The next instant a fantastic figure followed her—a man from whose waist hung a goatskin, and whose features were entirely hidden by a sort of mask made from a huge wolf's head, so that he looked like a monstrous, nightmare being, horribly

The Black Stone

compounded of elements both human and bestial. In his hand he held a bunch of long fir switches bound together at the larger ends, and the moonlight glinted on a chain of heavy gold looped about his neck.

A smaller chain depending from it suggested a pendant of some sort, but this was missing.

The people tossed their arms violently and seemed to redouble their shouts as this grotesque creature loped across the open space with many a fantastic leap and caper. Coming to the woman who lay before the monolith, he began to lash her with the switches he bore, and she leaped up and spun into the wild steps of the most incredible dance I have ever seen. And her tormentor danced with her, keeping the wild rhythm, matching her every shirl and bound, while incessantly raining cruel blows on her naked body. And at every blow he shouted a single word, over and over, and all the people shouted it back. I could see the working of their lips, and now the faint far-off murmur of their voices merged and blended into one distant shout, repeated over and over with slobbering ecstasy. But what the one word was, I could not make out.

In dizzy whirls spun the wild dancers, while the lookers-on, standing still in their tracks, followed the rhythm of their dance with swaying bodies and weaving arms. Madness grew in the eyes of the capering votaress and was reflected in the eyes of the watchers. Wilder and more extravagant grew the whirling frenzy of that mad dance—it became a bestial and obscene thing, while the old hag howled and battered the drum like a crazy woman, and the switches cracked out a devil's tune.

Blood trickled down the dancer's limbs but she seemed not to feel the lashing save as a stimulus for further enormities of outrageous motion; bounding into the midst of the yellow smoke which now spread out tenuous tentacles to embrace both flying figures, she seemed to merge with that foul fog and veil herself with it. Then emerging into plain view, closely followed by the beast-thing that flogged her, she shot into an indescrib-

The Black Stone

able, explosive burst of dynamic mad motion, and on the very crest of that mad wave, she dropped suddenly to the sward, quivering and panting as if completely overcome by her frenzied exertions. The lashing continued with unabated violence and intensity and she began to wriggle toward the monolith on her belly. The priest—or such I will call him—followed, lashing her unprotected body with all the power of his arm as she writhed along, leaving a heavy track of blood on the trampled earth. She reached the monolith, and gasping and panting, flung both arms about it and covered the cold stone with fierce hot kisses, as in frenzied and unholy adoration.

The fantastic priest bounded high in the air, flinging away the red-dabbled switches, and the worshippers, howling and foaming at the mouths, turned on each other with tooth and nail, rending one another's garments and flesh in a blind passion of bestiality. The priest swept up the infant with a long arm, and shouting again that Name, whirled the wailing babe high in the air and dashed its brains out against the monolith, leaving a ghastly stain on the black surface. Cold with horror I saw him rip the tiny body open with his bare brutish fingers and fling handfuls of blood on the shaft, then toss the red and torn shape into the brazier, extinguishing flame and smoke in a crimson rain, while the maddened brutes behind him howled over and over the Name. Then suddenly they all fell prostrate, writhing like snakes, while the priest flung wide his gory hands as in triumph. I opened my mouth to scream my horror and loathing, but only a dry rattle sounded; a huge monstrous toadlike thing squatted on the top of the monolith!

I saw its bloated, repulsive and unstable outline against the moonlight and set in what would have been the face of a natural creature, its huge, blinking eyes which reflected all the lust, abysmal greed, obscene cruelty and monstrous evil that has stalked the sons of men since their ancestors mowed blind and hairless in the tree-tops. In those grisly eyes were mirrored all the unholy things and vile secrets that sleep in the cities under the sea,

The Black Stone

and that skulk from the light of day in the blackness of primordial caverns. And so that ghastly thing that the unhallowed ritual and sadism and blood evoked from the silence of the hills, leered and blinked down on its bestial worshippers, who groveled in abhorrent abasement before it.

Now the beast-masked priest lifted the bound and weakly writhing girl in his brutish hands and held her up toward that horror on the monolith. And as that monstrosity sucked in its breath, lustfully and slobberingly, something snapped in my brain and I fell into a merciful faint.

I opened my eyes on a still white dawn. All the events of the night rushed back on me and I sprang up, then stared about me in amazement. The monolith brooded gaunt and silent above the sward which waved, green and untrampled, in the morning breeze. A few quick strides took me across the glade; here had the dancers leaped and bounded until the ground should have been trampled bare, and here had the votaress wriggled her painful way to the Stone, streaming blood on the earth. But no drop of crimson showed on the uncrushed sward. I looked, shudderingly, at the side of the monolith against which the bestial priest had brained the stolen baby—but no dark stain nor grisly clot showed there.

A dream! It had been a wild nightmare—or else—I shrugged my shoulders. What vivid clarity for a dream!

I returned quietly to the village and entered the inn without being seen. And there I sat meditating over the strange events of the night. More and more was I prone to discard the dream-theory. That what I had seen was illusion and without material substance, was evident. But I believed that I had looked on the mirrored shadow of a deed perpetrated in ghastly actuality in bygone days. But how was I to know? What proof to show that my vision had been a gathering of foul specters rather than a nightmare originating in my brain?

As if for answer a name flashed into my mind—Selim Bahadur! According to legend this man, who had

The Black Stone

been a soldier as well as a scribe, had commanded that part of Suleiman's army which had devastated Stregoicavar; it seemed logical enough; and if so, he had gone straight from the blotted-out countryside to the bloody field of Schomvaal, and his doom. I sprang up with a sudden shout—that manuscript which was taken from the Turk's body, and which Count Boris shuddered over— might it not contain some narration of what the conquering Turks found in Stregoicavar? What else could have shaken the iron nerves of the Polish adventurer? And since the bones of the Count had never been recovered, what more certain than that the lacquered case, with its mysterious contents, still lay hidden beneath the ruins that covered Boris Vladinoff? I began packing my bag with fierce haste.

Three days later found me esconced in a little village a few miles from the old battlefield, and when the moon rose I was working with savage intensity on the great pile of crumbling stone that crowned the hill. It was back-breaking toil—looking back now I cannot see how I accomplished it, though I labored without a pause from moonrise to dawn. Just as the sun was coming up I tore aside the last tangle of stones and looked on all that was mortal of Count Boris Vladinoff—only a few pitiful fragments of crumbling bone—and among them, crushed out of all original shape, lay a case whose lacquered surface had kept it from complete decay through the centuries.

I seized it with frenzied eagerness, and back in my tavern chamber I opened the case and found the parchment comparatively intact; and there was something else in the case—a small squat object wrapped in silk. I was wild to plumb the secrets of those yellowed pages, but weariness forbade me. Since leaving Stregoicavar I had hardly slept at all, and the terrific exertions of the previous night combined to overcome me. In spite of myself I was forced to stretch myself on my bed, nor did I awake until sundown.

The Black Stone

I snatched a hasty supper, and then in the light of a flickering candle, I set myself to read the near Turkish characters that covered the parchment. It was difficult work, for I am not deeply versed in the language and the archaic style of the narrative baffled me. But as I toiled through it a word or a phrase here and there leaped at me and a dimly growing horror shook me in its grip. I bent my energies fiercely to the task, and as the tale grew clearer and took more tangible form my blood chilled in my veins, my hair stood up and my tongue clove to my mouth.

At last when gray dawn was stealing through the latticed window, I laid down the manuscript and took up and unwrapped the thing in the bit of silk. Staring at it with haggard eyes I knew the truth of the matter was clinched, even had it been possible to doubt the veracity of that terrible manuscript.

And I replaced both obscene things in the case, nor did I rest or sleep or eat until that case containing them had been weighted with stones and flung into the deepest current of the Danube which, God grant, carried them back into the Hell from which they came.

It was no dream I dreamed on Midsummer Midnight in the hills above Stregoicavar. Well for Justin Geoffrey that he tarried there only in the sunlight and went his way, for had he gazed upon that ghastly conclave, his mad brain would have snapped before it did. How my own reason held, I do not know.

No—it was no dream—I gazed upon a foul rout of votaries long dead, come up from Hell to worship as of old; ghosts that bowed before a ghost. For Hell has long claimed their hideous god.

By what foul alchemy or godless sorcery the Gates of Hell are opened on that one eery night I do not know, but mine own eyes have seen. And I know I looked on no living thing that night, for the manuscript written in the careful hand of Selim Bahadur narrated at length what he and his raiders found in the valley of Stregoicavar; and I read, set down in detail, the blasphemous obscenities that

The Black Stone

torture wrung from the lips of screaming worshippers; and I read, too, of the lost, grim black cavern high in the hills where the horrified Turks hemmed a monstrous, bloated, wallowing toad-like being and slew it with flame and ancient steel blessed in old times by Muhammad, and with incantations that were old when Arabia was young. And even staunch old Selim's hand shook as he recorded the cataclysmic, earth-shaking death-howls of the monstrosity, which died not alone; for half-score of his slayers perished with him, in ways that Selim would not or could not describe.

And that squat idol carved of gold and wrapped in silk was an image of himself, and Selim tore it from the golden chain that looped the neck of the slain high priest of the mask.

Well that the Turks swept out that foul valley with torch and cleanly steel! Such sights as those brooding mountains have looked on belong to the darkness and abysses of lost eons. No—it is not fear of the toad-thing that makes me shudder in the night. He is made fast in Hell with his nauseous horde, freed only for an hour on the most weird night of the year, as I have seen. And of his worshippers, none remains.

But it is the realization that such things once crouched beastlike above the souls of men which brings cold sweat to my brow; and I fear to peer again into the leaves of Von Junzt's abomination. For now I understand his repeated phrase of keys!—aye! Keys to Outer Doors—links with an abhorrent past and—who knows?—of abhorrent spheres of the present. And I understand why the tavernkeeper's nightmare-haunted nephew saw in his dream, the Black Stone like a spire on a cyclopean black castle. If men ever excavate among those mountains they may find incredible things below those masking slopes. For the cave wherein the Turks trapped the—thing—was not truly a cavern, and I shudder to contemplate the gigantic gulf of eons which must stretch between this age and the time when the earth shook herself and reared up, like a wave, those blue mountains

The Black Stone

that, rising, enveloped unthinkable things. May no man ever seek to uproot that ghastly spire men call the Black Stone!

A Key! Aye, it is a Key, symbol of a forgotten horror. That horror has faded into the limbo from which it crawled, loathsomely, in the black dawn of the earth. But what of the other fiendish possibilities hinted at by Von Junzt—what of the monstrous hand which strangled out his life? Since reading what Selim Bahadur wrote, I can no longer doubt anything in the Black Book. Man was not always master of the earth—and is he now? What nameless shapes may even now lurk in the dark places of the world?

The Valley of the Worm

I will tell you of Niord and the Worm. You have heard the tale before in many guises wherein the hero was named Tyr, or Perseus, or Siegfried, or Beowulf, or Saint George. But it was Niord who met the loathly demoniac thing that crawled hideously up from Hell, and from which meeting sprang the cycle of hero-tales that revolves down the ages until the very substance of the truth is lost and passes into the limbo of all forgotten legends. I know whereof I speak, for I was Niord.

As I lie here awaiting death, which creeps slowly upon me like a blind slug, my dreams are filled with glittering visions and the pageantry of glory. It is not of the drab, disease-racked life of James Allison I dream, but all the gleaming figures of the mighty pageantry that have passed before, and shall come after; for I have faintly glimpsed, not merely the shapes that trail out behind, but shapes that come after, as a man in a long parade glimpses, far ahead, the line of figures that precede him winding over a distant hill, etched shadow-like against the sky. I am one and all the pageantry of shapes and guises and masks which have been, are, and shall be the visible manifestations of that illusive, intangible, but vitally existent spirit now promenading under the brief and temporary name of James Allison.

The Valley of the Worm

Each man on earth, each woman, is part and all of a similar caravan of shapes and beings. But they can not rememember—their minds can not bridge the brief, awful gulfs of blackness which lie between those unstable shapes, and which the spirit, soul or ego, in spanning, shakes off its fleshy masks. I remember. Why I can remember is the the strangest tale of all; but as I lie here with death's black wings slowly unfolding over me, all the dim folds of my previous lives are shaken out before my eyes, and I see myself in many forms and guises—braggart, swaggering, fearful, loving, foolish, all that men have been or will be.

I have been Man in many lands and many conditions; yet—and here is another strange thing—my line of reincarnation runs straight down one unerring channel. I have never been any but a man of that restless race men once called Nordheimr and later Aryans, and today name by many names and designations. Their history is my history, from the first mewling wail of a hairless white ape cub in the wastes of the arctic, to the death-cry of the last degenerate product of ultimate civilization, in some dim and unguessed future age.

My name has been Hialmar, Tyr, Bragi, Bran, Horsa, Eric, and John. I strode red-handed through the deserted streets of Rome behind the yellow-maned Brennus; I wandered through the violated plantations with Alaric and his Goths when the flame of burning villas lit the land like day and an empire was gasping its last under our sandalled feet; I waded sword in hand through the foaming surf from Hengist's galley to lay the foundations of England in blood and pillage; when Leif the Lucky sighted the broad white beaches of an unguessed world, I stood beside him in the bows of the dragonship, my golden beard blowing in the wind; and when Godfrey of Bouillon led his Crusaders over the walls of Jerusalem, I was among them in steel cap and brigandine.

But it is of none of these things I would speak. I would take you back with me into an age beside which

The Valley of the Worm

that of Brennus and Rome is as yesterday. I would take you back through, not merely centuries and millenniums, but epochs and dim ages unguessed by the wildest philosopher. Oh far, far and far will you fare into the nighted Past before you win beyond the boundaries of my race, blue-eyed, yellow-haired, wanderers, slayers, lovers, mightly in rapine and wayfaring.

It is the adventure of Niord Worm's-bane of which I speak—the root-stem of a whole cycle of hero-tales which has not yet reached its end, the grisly underlying reality that lurks behind time-distorted myths of dragons, fiends and monsters.

Yet it is not alone with the mouth of Niord that I will speak. I am James Allison no less than I was Niord, and as I unfold the tale, I will interpret some of his thoughts and dreams and deeds from the mouth of the modern I, so that the saga of Niord shall not be a meaningless chaos to you. His blood is your blood, who are sons of Aryan; but wide misty gulfs of eons lie horrifically between, and the deeds and dreams of Niord seem as alien to your deeds and dreams as the primordial and lion-haunted forest seems alien to the white-walled city street.

It was a strange world in which Niord lived and loved and fought, so long ago that even my eon-spanning memory can not recognize landmarks. Since then the surface of the earth has changed, not once but a score of times; continents have risen and sunk, seas have changed their beds and rivers their courses, glaciers have waxed and waned, and the very stars and constellations have altered and shifted.

It was so long ago that the cradle-land of my race was still in Nordheim. But the epic drifts of my people had already begun, and blue-eyed, yellow-maned tribes flowed eastward and southward and westward, on century-long treks that carried them around the world and left their bones and their traces in strange lands and wild waste places. On one of these drifts I grew from infancy to manhood. My knowledge of that northern homeland was dim memories, like half-remembered dreams, of blinding white snow plains and ice fields, of great fires roaring in the circle of hide tents, of yellow manes flying in great winds, and a sun setting in a lurid wallow of crimson clouds, blazing on trampled snow where still dark forms lay in pools that were redder than the sunset.

That last memory stands out clearer than the others. It was the field of Jotunheim, I was told in later years, whereon had just been fought that terrible battle which was the Armageddon of the Æsirfolk, the subject of a cycle of hero-songs for long ages, and which still lives today in dim dreams of Ragnarok and Goetterdaemmerung. I looked on that battle as a mewling infant; so I must have lived about—but I will not name the age, for I would be called a madman, and historians and geologists alike would rise to refute me.

But my memories of Nordheim were few and dim, paled by memories of that long, long trek upon which I had spent my life. We had not kept to a straight course, but our trend had been for ever southward. Sometimes we had bided for a while in fertile upland valleys or rich river-traversed plains, but always we took up the trail again, and not always because of drouth or famine. Often we left countries teeming with game and wild grain to push into wastelands. On our trail we moved endlessly, driven only by our restless whim, yet blindly following a cosmic law, the workings of which we never guessed, any more than the wild geese guess in their flights around the world. So at last we came into the Country of the Worm.

I will take up the tale at the time when we came into jungle-clad hills reeking with rot and teeming with spawning life, where the tom-toms of a savage people pulsed incessantly through the hot breathless night. These people came forth to dispute our way—short, strongly built men, black-haired, painted, ferocious, but indisputably white men. We knew their breed of old. They were Picts, and of all alien races the fiercest. We had met their kind before in thick forests, and in upland valleys beside

The Valley of the Worm

mountain lakes. But many moons had passed since those meetings.

I believe this particular tribe represented the easternmost drift of the race. They were the most primitive and ferocious of any I ever met. Already they were exhibiting hints of characteristics I have noted among black savages in jungle countries, though they had dwelt in these environs only a few generations. The abysmal jungle was engulfing them, was obliterating their pristine characteristics and shaping them in its own horrific mold. They were drifting into head-hunting, and cannibalism was but a step which I believe they must have taken before they became extinct. These things are natural adjuncts to the jungle; the Picts did not learn them from the black people, for then there were no blacks among those hills. In later years they came up from the south, and the Picts first enslaved and then were absorbed by them. But with that my saga of Niord is not concerned.

We came into that brutish hill country, with its squalling abysms of savagery and black primitiveness. We were a whole tribe marching on foot, old men, wolfish with their long beards and gaunt limbs, giant warriors in their prime, naked children running along the line of march, women with tousled yellow locks carrying babies which never cried—unless it were to scream from pure rage. I do not remember our numbers, except that there were some five hundred fighting-men—and by fighting-men I mean all males, from the child just strong enough to lift a bow, to the oldest of the old men. In that madly ferocious age all were fighters. Our women fought, when brought to bay, like tigresses, and I have seen a babe, not yet old enough to stammer articulate words, twist its head and sink its tiny teeth in the foot that stamped out its life.

Oh, we were fighters! Let me speak of Niord. I am proud of him, the more when I consider the paltry crippled body of James Allison, the unstable mask I now wear. Niord was tall, with great shoulders, lean hips and mighty limbs. His muscles were long and swelling, denoting endurance and speed as well as strength. He could run all day without tiring, and he possessed a co-ordination that made his movements a blur of blinding speed. If I told you his full strength, you would brand me a liar. But there is no man on earth today strong enough to bend the bow Niord handled with ease. The longest arrow-flight on record is that of a Turkish archer who sent a shaft 482 yards. There was not a stripling in my tribe who could not have bettered that flight.

As we entered the jungle country we heard the tom-toms booming across the mysterious valleys that slumbered between the brutish hills, and in a broad, open plateau we met our enemies. I do not believe these Picts knew us, even by legends, or they had never rushed so openly to the onset, though they outnumbered us. But there was no attempt at ambush. They swarmed out of the trees, dancing and singing their war-songs, yelling their barbarous threats. Our heads should hang in their idol-hut and our yellow-haired women should bear their sons. Ho! ho! ho! By Ymir, it was Niord who laughed then, not James Allison. Just so we of the Æsir laughed to hear their threats—deep thunderous laughter from broad and mighty chests. Our trail was laid in blood and embers through many lands. We were the slayers and ravishers, striding sword in hand across the world, and that these folk threatened us woke our rugged humor.

We went to meet them, naked but for our wolfhides, swinging our bronze swords, and our singing was like rolling thunder in the hills. They sent their arrows among us, and we gave back their fire. They could not match us in archery. Our arrows hissed in blinding clouds among them, dropping them like autumn leaves, until they howled and frothed like mad dogs and charged to hand-grips. And we, mad with the fighting joy, dropped our bows and ran to meet them, as a lover runs to his love.

By Ymir, it was a battle to madden and make drunken with the slaughter and the fury. The Picts were as ferocious as we, but ours was the superior physique, the keener wit, the more highly developed fighting-brain. We won because we were a superior race, but it was no easy victory. Corpses littered the blood-soaked earth; but at last they broke, and we cut them down as they ran, to the very edge of the trees. I tell of that fight in a few bald words. I can not paint the madness, the reek of sweat and blood, the panting, muscle-straining effort, the splintering of bones under mighty blows, the rending and hewing of quivering sentient flesh; above all the merciless abysmal savagery of the whole affair, in which there was neither rule nor order, each man fighting as he would or could. If I might do so, you would recoil in horror; even the modern I, cognizant of my close kinship with those times, stand aghast as I review that butchery. Mercy was yet unborn, save as some individual's whim, and rules of warfare were as yet undreamed of. It was an age in which each tribe and each human fought tooth and fang from birth to death, and neither gave nor expected mercy.

So we cut down the fleeing Picts, and our women came out on the field to brain the wounded enemies with stones, or cut their throats with copper knives. We did not torture. We were no more cruel than life demanded. The rule of life was ruthlessness, but there is more wanton cruelty today than ever we dreamed of. It was not wanton bloodthirstiness that made us butcher wounded and captive foes. It was because we knew our chances of survival increased with each enemy slain.

Yet there was occasionally a touch of individual mercy, and so it was in this fight. I had been occupied with a duel with an especially valiant enemy. His tousled thatch of black hair scarcely came above my chin, but he was a solid knot of steel-spring muscles, than which lightning scarcely moved faster. He had an iron sword and a hide-covered buckler. I had a knotty-headed bludgeon. That fight was one that glutted even my battle-lusting soul. I was bleeding from a score of flesh wounds before one of my terrible, lashing strokes smashed his shield like cardboard, and an instant later my bludgeon glanced from his unprotected head. Ymir! Even now I stop to laugh and marvel at the hardness of that

The Valley of the Worm

Pict's skull. Men of that age were assuredly built on a rugged plan! That blow should have spattered his brains like water. It did lay his scalp open horribly, dashing him senseless to the earth, where I let him lie, supposing him to be dead, as I joined in the slaughter of the fleeing warriors.

When I returned reeking with sweat and blood, my club horridly clotted with blood and brains, I noticed that my antagonist was regaining consciousness, and that a naked tousle-headed girl was preparing to give him the finishing touch with a stone she could scarcely lift. A vagrant whim caused me to check the blow. I had enjoyed the fight, and I admired the adamantine quality of his skull.

We made camp a short distance away, burned our dead on a great pyre, and after looting the corpses of the enemy, we dragged them across the plateau and cast them down in a valley to make a feast for the hyenas, jackals and vultures which were already gathering. We kept close watch that night, but we were not attacked, though far away through the jungle we could make out the red gleam of fires, and could faintly hear, when the wind veered, the throb of tom-toms and demoniac screams and yells—keenings for the slain or mere animal squallings of fury.

Nor did they attack us in the days that followed. We bandaged our captive's wounds and quickly learned his primitive tongue, which, however, was so different from ours that I can not conceive of the two languages having ever had a common source.

His name was Grom, and he was a great hunter and fighter, he boasted. He talked freely and held no grudge, grinning broadly and showing tusk-like teeth, his beady eyes glittering from under the tangled black mane that fell over his low forehead. His limbs were almost ape-like in their thickness.

He was vastly interested in his captors, though he could never understand why he had been spared; to the end it remained an inexplicable mystery to him. The Picts obeyed the law of survival even more rigidly than did the

The Valley of the Worm

Æsir. They were the more practical, as shown by their more settled habits. They never roamed as far or as blindly as we. Yet in every line we were the superior race.

Grom, impressed by our intelligence and fighting qualities, volunteered to go into the hills and make peace for us with his people. It was immaterial to us, but we let him go. Slavery had not yet been dreamed of.

So Grom went back to his people, and we forgot about him, except that I went a trifle more cautiously about my hunting, expecting him to be lying in wait to put an arrow through my back. Then one day we heard a rattle of tom-toms, and Grom appeared at the edge of the jungle, his face split in his gorilla-grin, with the painted, skin-clad, feather-bedecked chiefs of the clans. Our ferocity had awed them, and our sparing of Grom further impressed them. They could not understand leniency; evidently we valued them too cheaply to bother about killing one when he was in our power.

So peace was made with much pow-wow, and sworn to with many strange oaths and rituals—we swore only by Ymir, and an Æsir never broke that vow. But they swore by the elements, by the idol which sat in the fetish-hut where fires burned for ever and a withered crone slapped a leather-covered drum all night long, and by another being too terrible to be named.

Then we all sat around the fires and gnawed meatbones, and drank a fiery concoction they brewed from wild grain, and the wonder is that the feast did not end in a general massacre; for that liquor had devils in it and made maggots writhe in our brains. But no harm came of our vast drunkenness, and thereafter we dwelt at peace with our barbarous neighbors. They taught us many things, and learned many more from us. But they taught us iron-workings, into which they had been forced by the lack of copper in those hills, and we quickly excelled them.

We went freely among their villages—mud-walled clusters of huts in hilltop clearings, overshadowed by giant trees—and we allowed them to come at will among

The Valley of the Worm

our camps—straggling lines of hide tents on the plateau where the battle had been fought. Our young men cared not for their squat beady-eyed women, and our rangy clean-limbed girls with their tousled yellow heads were not drawn to the hairy-breasted savages. Familiarity over a period of years would have reduced the repulsion on either side, until the two races would have flowed together to form one hybrid people, but long before that time the Æsir rose and departed, vanishing into the mysterious hazes of the haunted south. But before that exodus there came to pass the horror of the Worm.

I hunted with Grom and he led me into brooding, uninhabited valleys and up into silence-haunted hills where no men had set foot before us. But there was one valley, off in the mazes of the southwest, into which he would not go. Stumps of shattered columns, relics of a forgotten civilization, stood among the trees on the valley floor. Grom showed them to me, as we stood on the cliffs that flanked the mysterious vale, but he would not go down into it, and he dissuaded me when I would have gone alone. He would not speak plainly of the danger that lurked there, but it was greater than that of serpent or tiger, or the trumpeting elephants which occasionally wandered up in devastating droves from the south.

Of all beasts, Grom told me in the gutturals of his tongue, the Picts feared only Satha, the great snake, and they shunned the jungle where he lived. But there was another thing they feared, and it was connected in some manner with the Valley of Broken Stones, as the Picts called the crumbling pillars. Long ago, when his ancestors had first come into the country, they had dared that grim vale, and a whole clan of them had perished, suddenly, horribly, and unexplainably. At least Grom did not explain. The horror had come up out of earth, somehow, and it was not good to talk of it, since it was believed that It might be summoned by speaking of It—whatever It was.

But Grom was ready to hunt with me anywhere else;

The Valley of the Worm

for he was the greatest hunter among the Picts, and many and fearful were our adventures. Once I killed, with the iron sword I had forged with my own hands, that most terrible of all beasts—old saber-tooth, which men today call a tiger because he was more like a tiger than anything else. In reality he was almost as much like a bear in build, save for his unmistakably feline head. Saber-tooth was massive-limbed, with a low-hung, great, heavy body, and he vanished from the earth because he was too terrible a fighter, even for that grim age. As his muscles and ferocity grew, his brain dwindled until at last even the instinct of self-preservation vanished. Nature, who maintains her balance in such things, destroyed him because, had his super-fighting powers been allied with an intelligent brain, he would have destroyed all other forms of life on earth. He was a freak on the road of evolution—organic development gone mad and run to fangs and talons, to slaughter and destruction.

I killed saber-tooth in a battle that would make a saga in itself, and for months afterward I lay semi-delirious with ghastly wounds that made the toughest warriors shake their heads. The Picts said that never before had a man killed a saber-tooth single-handed. Yet I recovered, to the wonder of all.

While I lay at the doors of death there was a secession from the tribe. It was a peaceful secession, such as continually occurred and contributed greatly to the peopling of the world by yellow-haired tribes. Forty-five of the young men took themselves mates simultaneously and wandered off to found a clan of their own. There was no revolt; it was a racial custom which bore fruits in all the later ages, when tribes sprung from the same roots met, after centuries of separation, and cut one another's throats with joyous abandon. The tendency of the Aryan and the pre-Aryan was always toward disunity, clans splitting off the main stem, and scattering.

So these young men, led by one Bragi, my brother-in-arms, took their girls and venturing to the southwest, took up their abode in the Valley of Broken

The Valley of the Worm

Stones. The Picts expostulated, hinting vaguely of a monstrous doom that haunted the vale, but the Æsir laughed. We had left our own demons and weirds in the icy wastes of the far blue north, and the devils of other races did not much impress us.

When my full strength was returned, and the grisly wounds were only scars, I girt on my weapons and strode over the plateau to visit Bragi's clan. Grom did not accompany me. He had not been in the Æsir camp for several days. But I knew the way. I remembered well the valley, from the cliffs of which I had looked down and seen the lake at the upper end, the trees thickening into forest at the lower extremity. The sides of the valley were high sheer cliffs, and a steep broad ridge at either end cut it off from the surrounding country. It was toward the lower or southwestern end that the valley-floor was dotted thickly with ruined columns, some towering high among the trees, some fallen into heaps of lichen-clad stones. What race reared them none knew. But Grom had hinted fearsomely of a hairy, apish monstrosity dancing loathsomely under the moon to a demoniac piping that induced horror and madness.

I crossed the plateau whereon our camp was pitched, descended the slope, traversed a shallow vegetation-choked valley, climbed another slope, and plunged into the hills. A half-day's leisurely travel brought me to the ridge on the other side of which lay the valley of the pillars. For many miles I had seen no sign of human life. The settlements of the Picts all lay many miles to the east. I topped the ridge and looked down into the dreaming valley with its still blue lake, its brooding cliffs and its broken columns jutting among the trees. I looked for smoke. I saw none, but I saw vultures wheeling in the sky over a cluster of tents on the lake shore.

I came down the ridge warily and approached the silent camp. In it I halted, frozen with horror. I was not easily moved. I had seen death in many forms, and had fled from or taken part in red massacres that spilled blood

The Valley of the Worm

like water and heaped the earth with corpses. But here I was confronted with an organic devastation that staggered and appalled me. Of Bragi's embryonic clan, not one remained alive, and not one corpse was whole. Some of the hide tents still stood erect. Others were mashed down and flattened out, as if crushed by some monstrous weight, so that at first I wondered if a drove of elephants had stampeded across the camp. But no elephants ever wrought such destruction as I saw strewn on the bloody ground. The camp was a shambles, littered with bits of flesh and fragments of bodies—hands, feet, heads, pieces of human debris. Weapons lay about, some of them stained with a greenish slime like that which spurts from a crushed caterpillar.

No human foe could have committed this ghastly atrocity. I looked at the lake, wondering if nameless amphibian monsters had crawled from the calm waters whose deep blue told of unfathomed depths. Then I saw a print left by the destroyer. It was a track such as a titanic worm might leave, yards broad, winding back down the valley. The grass lay flat where it ran, and bushes and small trees had been crushed down into the earth, all horribly smeared with blood and greenish slime.

With berserk fury in my soul I drew my sword and started to follow it, when a call attracted me. I wheeled, to see a stocky form approaching me from the ridge. It was Grom the Pict, and when I think of the courage it must have taken for him to have overcome all the instincts planted in him by traditional teachings and personal experience, I realize the full depths of his friendship for me.

Squatting on the lake shore, spear in his hands, his black eyes ever roving fearfully down the brooding tree-waving reaches of the valley, Grom told me of the horror that had come upon Bragi's clan under the moon. But first he told me of it, as his sires had told the tale to him.

Long ago the Picts had drifted down from the northwest on a long, long trek, finally reaching these

The Valley of the Worm

jungle-covered hills, where, because they were weary, and because the game and fruit were plentiful and there were no hostile tribes, they halted and built their mud-walled villages.

Some of them, a whole clan of that numerous tribe, took up their abode in the Valley of the Broken Stones. They found the columns and a great ruined temple back in the trees, and in that temple there was no shrine or altar, but the mouth of a shaft that vanished deep into the black earth, and in which there were no steps such as a human being would make and use. They built their village in the valley, and in the night, under the moon, horror came upon them and left only broken walls and bits of slime-smeared flesh.

In those days the Picts feared nothing. The warriors of the other clans gathered and sang their war-songs and danced their war-dances, and followed a broad track of blood and slime to the shaft-mouth in the temple. They howled defiance and hurled down boulders which were never heard to strike bottom. Then began a thin demoniac piping, and up from the well pranced a hideous anthropomorphic figure dancing to the weird strains of a pipe it held in its monstrous hands. The horror of its aspect froze the fierce Picts with amazement, and close behind it a vast white bulk heaved up from the subterranean darkness. Out of the shaft came a slavering mad nightmare which arrows pierced but could not check, which swords carved but could not slay. It fell slobbering upon the warriors, crushing them to crimson pulp, tearing them to bits as an octopus might tear small fishes, sucking their blood from their mangled limbs and devouring them even as they screamed and struggled. The survivors fled, pursued to the very ridge, up which, apparently, the monster could not propel its quaking mountainous bulk.

After that they did not dare the silent valley. But the dead came to their shamans and old men in dreams and told them strange and terrible secrets. They spoke of an ancient, ancient race of semihuman beings which once

The Valley of the Worm

inhabited that valley and reared those columns for their own weird inexplicable purposes. The white monster in the pits was their god, summoned up from the nighted abysses of mid-earth uncounted fathoms below the black mold, by sorcery unknown to the sons of men. The hairy anthropomorphic being was its servant, created to serve the god, a formless elemental spirit drawn up from below and cased in flesh, organic but beyond the understanding of humanity. The Old Ones had long vanished into the limbo from whence they crawled in the black dawn of the universe, but their bestial god and his inhuman slave lived on. Yet both were organic after a fashion, and could be wounded, though no human weapon had been found potent enough to slay them.

Bragi and his clan had dwelt for weeks in the valley before the horror struck. Only the night before, Grom, hunting above the cliffs, and by that token daring greatly, had been paralyzed by a high-pitched demon piping, and then by a mad clamor of human screaming. Stretched face down in the dirt, hiding his head in a tangle of grass, he had not dared to move, even when the shrieks died away in the slobbering, repulsive sounds of a hideous feast. When dawn broke he had crept shuddering to the cliffs to look down into the valley, and the sight of the devastation, even when seen from afar, had driven him in yammering flight far into the hills. But it had occurred to him, finally, that he should warn the rest of the tribe, and returning, on his way to the camp on the plateau, he had seen me entering the valley.

So spoke Grom, while I sat and brooded darkly, my chin on my mighty fist. I can not frame in modern words the clan-feeling that in those days was a living vital part of every man and woman. In a world where talon and fang were lifted on every hand, and the hands of all men raised against an individual, except those of his own clan, tribal instinct was more than the phrase it is today. It was as much a part of a man as was his heart or his right hand. This was necessary, for only thus banded together in unbreakable groups could mankind have survived in the terrible environments of the primitive world. So now the personal grief I felt for Bragi and the clean-limbed young men and laughing white-skinned girls was drowned in a deeper sea of grief and fury that was cosmic in its depth and intensity. I sat grimly, while the Pict squatted anxiously beside me, his gaze roving from me to the menacing deeps of the valley where the accursed columns loomed like broken teeth of cackling hags among the waving leafy reaches.

I, Niord, was not one to use my brain over-much. I lived in a physical world, and there were the old men of the tribe to do my thinking. But I was one of a race destined to become dominant mentally as well as physically, and I was no mere muscular animal. So as I sat there there came dimly and then clearly a thought to me that brought a short fierce laugh from my lips.

Rising, I bade Grom aid me, and we built a pyre on the lake shore of dried wood, the ridge-poles of the tents, and the broken shafts of spears. Then we collected the grisly fragments that had been parts of Bragi's band, and we laid them on the pile, and struck flint and steel to it.

The thick sad smoke crawled serpent-like into the sky, and turning to Grom, I made him guide me to the jungle where lurked that scaly horror, Satha, the great serpent. Grom gaped at me; not the greatest hunters among the Picts sought out the mighty crawling one. But my will was like a wind that swept him along my course, and at last he led the way. We left the valley by the upper end, crossing the ridge, skirting the tall cliffs, and plunged into the fastnesses of the south, which was peopled only by the grim denizens of the jungle. Deep into the jungle we went, until we came to a low-lying expanse, dank and dark beneath the great creeper-festooned trees, where our feet sank deep into the spongy silt, carpeted by rotting vegetation, and slimy moisture oozed up beneath their pressure. This, Grom told me, was the realm haunted by Satha, the great serpent.

Let me speak of Satha. There is nothing like him on earth today, nor has there been for countless ages. Like

The Valley of the Worm

the meat-eating dinosaur, like old saber-tooth, he was too terrible to exist. Even then he was a survival of a grimmer age when life and its forms were cruder and more hideous. There were not many of his kind then, though they may have existed in great numbers in the reeking ooze of the vast jungle-tangled swamps still farther south. He was larger than any python of modern ages, and his fangs dripped with poison a thousand times more deadly than that of a king cobra.

He was never worshipped by the pure-blood Picts, though the blacks that came later deified him, and that adoration persisted in the hybrid race that sprang from the Negroes and their white conquerors. But to other peoples he was the nadir of evil horror, and tales of him became twisted into demonology; so in later ages Satha became the veritable devil of the white races, and the Stygians first worshipped, and then, when they became Egyptians, abhorred him under the name of Set, the Old Serpent, while to the Semites he became Leviathan and Satan. He was terrible enough to be a god, for he was a crawling death. I had seen a bull elephant fall dead in his tracks from Satha's bite. I had seen him, had glimpsed him writhing his horrific way through the dense jungle, had seen him take his prey, but I had never hunted him. He was too grim, even for the slayer of old saber-tooth.

But now I hunted him, plunging farther and farther into the hot, breathless reek of his jungle, even when friendship for me could not drive Grom farther. He urged me to paint my body and sing my death-song before I advanced farther, but I pushed on unheeding.

In a natural runway that wound between the shouldering trees, I set a trap. I found a large tree, soft and spongy of fiber, but thick-boled and heavy, and I hacked through its base close to the ground with my great sword, directing its fall so that when it toppled, its top crashed into the branches of a smaller tree, leaving it leaning across the runway, one end resting on the earth, the other caught in the small tree. Then I cut away the branches on the under side, and cutting a slim tough sapling I trimmed

The Valley of the Worm

it and stuck it upright like a prop-pole under the leaning tree. Then, cutting away the tree which supported it, I left the great trunk poised precariously on the prop-pole, to which I fastened a long vine, as thick as my wrist.

Then I went alone through that primordial twilight jungle until an overpowering fetid odor assailed my nostrils, and from the rank vegetation in front of me, Satha reared up his hideous head, swaying lethally from side to side, while his forked tongue jetted in and out, and his great yellow terrible eyes burned icily on me with all the evil wisdom of the black elder world that was when man was not. I backed away, feeling no fear, only an icy sensation along my spine, and Satha came sinuously after me, his shining eighty-foot barrel rippling over the rotting vegetation in mesmeric silence. His wedge-shaped head was bigger than the head of the hugest stallion, his trunk was thicker than a man's body, and his scales shimmered with a thousand changing scintillations. I was to Satha as a mouse is to a king cobra, but I was fanged as no mouse ever was. Quick as I was, I knew I could not avoid the lightning stroke of that great triangular head; so I dared not let him come too close. Subtly I fled down the runway, and behind me the rush of the great supple body was like the sweep of wind through the grass.

He was not far behind me when I raced beneath the deadfall, and as the great shining length glided under the trap, I gripped the vine with both hands and jerked desperately. With a crash the great trunk fell across Satha's scaly back, some six feet back of his wedge-shaped head.

I had hoped to break his spine but I do not think it did, for the great body coiled and knotted, the mighty tail lashed and thrashed, mowing down the bushes as if with a giant flail. At the instant of the fall, the huge head had whipped about and struck the tree with a terrific impact, the mighty fangs shearing through bark and wood like scimitars. Now, as if aware he fought an inanimate foe, Satha turned on me, standing out of his reach. The scaly neck writhed and arched, the mighty jaws gaped,

The Valley of the Worm

disclosing fangs a foot in length, from which dripped venom that might have burned through solid stone.

I believe, what of his stupendous strength, that Satha would have writhed from under the trunk, but for a broken branch that had been driven deep into his side, holding him like a barb. The sound of his hissing filled the jungle and his eyes glared at me with such concentrated evil that I shook despite myself. Oh, he knew it was I who had trapped him! Now I came as close as I dared, and with a sudden powerful cast of my spear, transfixed his neck just below the gaping jaws, nailing him to the tree-trunk. Then I dared greatly, for he was far from dead, and I knew he would in an instant tear the spear from the wood and be free to strike. But in that instant I ran in, and swinging my sword with all my great power, I hewed off his terrible head.

The heavings and contortions of Satha's prisoned form in life were naught to the convulsions of his headless length in death. I retreated, dragging the gigantic head after me with a crooked pole, and at a safe distance from the lashing, flying tail, I set to work. I worked with naked death then, and no man ever toiled more gingerly than did I. For I cut out the poison sacs at the base of the great fangs, and in the terrible venom I soaked the heads of eleven arrows, being careful that only the bronze points were in the liquid, which else had corroded away the wood of the tough shafts. While I was doing this, Grom, driven by comradeship and curiosity, came stealing nervously through the jungle, and his mouth gaped as he looked on the head of Satha.

For hours I steeped the arrowheads in the poison, until they were caked with a horrible green scum, and showed tiny flecks of corrosion where the venom had eaten into the solid bronze. I wrapped them carefully in broad, thick, rubber-like leaves, and then, though night had fallen and the hunting beasts were roaring on every hand, I went back through the jungled hills, Grom with me, until at dawn we came again to the high cliffs that loomed above the Valley of Broken Stones.

The Valley of the Worm

At the mouth of the valley I broke my spear, and I took all the unpoisoned shafts from my quiver, and snapped them. I painted my face and limbs as the Æsir painted themselves only when they went forth to certain doom, and I sang my death-song to the sun as it rose over the cliffs, my yellow mane blowing in the morning wind.

Then I went down into the valley, bow in hand.

Grom could not drive himself to follow me. He lay on his belly in the dust and howled like a dying dog.

I passed the lake and the silent camp where the pyre-ashes still smoldered, and came under the thickening trees beyond. About me the columns loomed, mere shapeless heaps from the ravages of staggering eons. The trees grew more dense, and under their vast leafy branches the very light was dusky and evil. As in twilight shadow I saw the ruined temple, cyclopean walls staggering up from masses of decaying masonry and fallen blocks of stone. About six hundred yards in front of it a great column reared up in an open glade, eighty or ninety feet in height. It was so worn and pitted by weather and time that any child of my tribe could have climbed it, and I marked it and changed my plan.

I came to the ruins and saw huge crumbling walls upholding a domed roof from which many stones had fallen, so that it seemed like the lichen-grown ribs of some mythical monster's skeleton arching above me. Titanic columns flanked the open doorway through which ten elephants could have stalked abreast. Once there might have been inscriptions and hieroglyphics on the pillars and walls, but they were long worn away. Around the great room, on the inner side, ran columns in better state of preservation. On each of these columns was a flat pedestal, and some dim instinctive memory vaguely resurrected a shadowy scene wherein black drums roared madly, and on these pedestals monstrous beings squatted loathsomely in inexplicable rituals rooted in the black dawn of the universe.

There was no altar—only the mouth of a great well-like shaft in the stone floor, with strange obscene

The Valley of the Worm

carvings all about the rim. I tore great pieces of stone from the rotting floor and cast them down the shaft which slanted down into utter darkness. I heard them bound along the side, but I did not hear them strike bottom. I cast down stone after stone, each with a searing curse, and at last I heard a sound that was not the dwindling rumble of the falling stones. Up from the well floated a weird demon-piping that was a symphony of madness. Far down in the darkness I glimpsed the faint fearful glimmering of a vast white bulk.

I retreated slowly as the piping grew louder, falling back through the broad doorway. I heard a scratching, scrambling noise, and up from the shaft and out of the doorway between the colossal columns came a prancing incredible figure. It went erect like a man, but it was covered with fur, that was shaggiest where its face should have been. If it had ears, nose and a mouth I did not discover them. Only a pair of staring red eyes leered from the furry mask. Its misshapen hands held a strange set of pipes, on which it blew weirdly as it pranced toward me with many a grotesque caper and leap.

Behind it I heard a repulsive obscene noise as of a quaking unstable mass heaving up out of a well. Then I nocked an arrow, drew the cord and sent the shaft singing through the furry breast of the dancing monstrosity. It went down as though struck by a thunderbolt, but to my horror the piping continued, though the pipes had fallen from the malformed hands. Then I turned and ran fleetly to the column, up which I swarmed before I looked back. When I reached the pinnacle I looked, and because of the shock and surprise of what I saw, I almost fell from my dizzy perch.

Out of the temple the monstrous deweller in the darkness had come, and I, who had expected a horror yet cast in some terrestrial mold, looked on the spawn of nightmare. From what subterranean hell it crawled in the long ago I know not, nor what black age it represented. But it was not a beast, as humanity knows beasts. I call it a worm for lack of a better term. There is no earthly

The Valley of the Worm

language which has a name for it. I can only say that it looked somewhat more like a worm than it did an octopus, a serpent or a dinosaur.

It was white and pulpy, and drew its quaking bulk along the ground, worm-fashion. But it had wide flat tentacles, and fleshy feelers, and other adjuncts the use of which I am unable to explain. And it had a long proboscis which it curled and uncurled like an elephant's trunk. Its forty eyes, set in a horrific circle, were composed of thousands of facets of as many scintillant colors which changed and altered in never-ending transmutation. But through all interplay of hue and glint, they retained their evil intelligence—intelligence there was behind those flickering facets, not human nor yet bestial, but a night-born demoniac intelligence such as men in dreams vaguely sense throbbing titanically in the black gulfs outside our material universe. In size the monster was mountainous; its bulk would have dwarfed a mastodon.

But even as I shook with the cosmic horror of the thing, I drew a feathered shaft to my ear and arched it singing on its way. Grass and bushes were crushed flat as the monster came toward me like a moving mountain and shaft after shaft I sent with terrific force and deadly precision. I could not miss so huge a target. The arrows sank to the feathers or clear out of sight in the unstable bulk, each bearing enough poison to have stricken dead a bull elephant. Yet on it came, swiftly, appallingly, apparently heedless of both the shafts and the venom in which they were steeped. And all the time the hideous music played a maddening accompaniment, whining thinly from the pipes that lay untouched on the ground.

My confidence faded; even the poison of Satha was futile against this uncanny being. I drove my last shaft almost straight downward into the quaking white mountain, so close was the monster under my perch. Then suddenly its color altered. A wave of ghastly blue surged over it, and the vast bulk heaved in earthquake-like convulsions. With a terrible plunge it struck the lower part of the column, which crashed to falling shards of

The Valley of the Worm

stone. But even with the impact, I leaped far out and fell through the empty air full upon the monster's back.

The spongy skin yielded and gave beneath my feet, and I drove my sword hilt-deep, dragging it through the pulpy flesh, ripping a horrible yard-long wound, from which oozed a green slime. Then a flip of a cable-like tentacle flicked me from the titan's back and spun me three hundred feet through the air to crash among a cluster of giant trees.

The impact must have splintered half the bones in my frame, for when I sought to grasp my sword again and crawl anew to the combat, I could not move hand or foot, could only writhe helplessly with my broken back. But I could see the monster and I knew that I had won, even in defeat. The mountainous bulk was heaving and billowing, the tentacles were lashing madly, the antennae writhing and knotting, and the nauseous whiteness had changed to a pale and grisly green. It turned ponderously and lurched back toward the temple, rolling like a crippled ship in a heavy swell. Trees crashed and splintered as it lumbered against them.

I wept with pure fury because I could not catch up my sword and rush in to die glutting my berserk madness in mighty strokes. But the worm-god was death-stricken and needed not my futile sword. The demon pipes on the ground kept up their infernal tune, and it was like the fiend's death-dirge. Then as the monster veered and floundered, I saw it catch up the corpse of its hairy slave. For an instant the apish form dangled in midair, gripped round by the trunk-like proboscis, then was dashed against the temple wall with a force that reduced the hairy body to a mere shapeless pulp. At that the pipes screamed out horribly, and fell silent for ever.

The titan staggered on the brink of the shaft; then another change came over it—a frightful transfiguration the nature of which I can not yet describe. Even now when I try to think of it clearly, I am only chaotically conscious of a blasphemous, unnatural transmutation of form and substance, shocking and indescribable. Then the strangely altered bulk tumbled into the shaft to roll down into the ultimate darkness from whence it came, and I knew that it was dead. And as it vanished into the well, with a rending, grinding groan the ruined walls quivered from dome to base. They bent inward and buckled with deafening reverberation, the columns splintered, and with a cataclysmic crash the dome itself came thundering down. For an instant the air seemed veiled with flying debris and stone-dust, through which the treetops lashed madly as in a storm or an earthquake convulsion. Then all was clear again and I stared, shaking the blood from my eyes. Where the temple had stood there lay only a colossal pile of shattered masonry and broken stones, and every column in the valley had fallen, to lie in crumbling shards.

In the silence that followed I heard Grom wailing a dirge over me. I bade him lay my sword in my hand, and he did so, and bent close to hear what I had to say, for I was passing swiftly.

"Let my tribe remember," I said, speaking slowly. "Let the tale be told from village to village, from camp to camp, from tribe to tribe, so that men may know that not man nor beast nor devil may prey in safety on the golden-haired people of Asgard. Let them build me a cairn where I lie and lay me therein with my bow and sword at hand, to guard this valley for ever; so if the ghost of the god I slew comes up from below, my ghost will ever be ready to give it battle."

And while Grom howled and beat his hairy breast, death came to me in the Valley of the Worm.

Wolfshead

Fear? your pardon, Messieurs, but the meaning of fear you do not know. No, I hold to my statement. You are soldiers, adventurers. You have known the charges of regiments of dragoons, the frenzy of wind-lashed seas. But fear, real hair-raising, horror-crawling fear, you have not known. I myself have known such fear; but until the legions of darkness swirl from hell's gate and the world flames to ruin, will never such fear again be known to men.

Hark, I will tell you the tale; for it was many years ago and half across the world, and none of you will ever see the man of whom I tell you, or seeing, know.

Return, then, with me across the years to a day when I, a reckless young cavalier, stepped from the small boat that had landed me from the ship floating in the harbor, cursed the mud that littered the crude wharf, and strode up the landing toward the castle, in answer to the invitation of an old friend, Dom Vincente da Lusto.

Dom Vincente was a strange, far-sighted man—a strong man, one who saw visions beyond the ken of his time. In his veins, perhaps, ran the blood of those old Phoenicians who, the priests tell us, ruled the seas and built cities in far lands, in the dim ages. His plan of fortune was strange and yet successful; few men would have

Wolfshead

thought of it; fewer could have succeeded. For his estate was upon the western coast of that dark, mystic continent, that baffler of explorers—Africa.

There by a small bay had he cleared away the sullen jungle, built his castle and his storehouses, and with ruthless hand had he wrested the riches of the land. Four ships he had: three smaller craft and one great galleon. These plied between his domains and the cities of Spain, Portugal, France, and even England, laden with rare woods, ivory, slaves; the thousand strange riches that Dom Vincente had gained by trade and by conquest.

Aye, a wild venture, a wilder commerce. And yet might he have shaped an empire from the dark land, had it not been for the rat faced Carlos, his nephew—but I run ahead of my tale.

Look, Messieurs, I draw a map on the table, thus, with finger dipped in wine. Here lay the small, shallow harbor, and here the wide wharves. A landing ran thus, up the slight slope with hutlike warehouses on each side, and here it stopped at a wide, shallow moat. Over it went a narrow drawbridge and then one was confronted with a high palisade of logs set in the ground. This extended entirely around the castle. The castle itself was built on the model of another, earlier age; being more for strength then beauty. Built of stone brought from a great distance; years of labor and a thousand Negroes toiling beneath the lash had reared its walls, and now, completely, it offered an almost impregnable appearance. Such was the intention of its builders, for Barbary pirates ranged the coasts, and the horror of a native uprising lurked ever near.

A space of about a half-mile on every side of the castle was kept cleared away and roads had been built through the marshy land. All this had required an immense amount of labor, but manpower was plentiful. A present to a chief, and he furnished all that was needed. And Portuguese know how to make men work!

Less than three hundred yards to the east of the

Wolfshead

castle ran a wide, shallow river, which emptied into the harbor. The name has entirely slipt my mind. It was a heathenish title and I could never lay my tongue to it.

I found that I was not the only friend invited to the castle. It seems that once a year or some such matter, Dom Vincente brought a host of jolly companions to his lonely estate and made merry for some weeks, to make up for the work and solitude of the rest of the year.

In fact, it was nearly night, and a great banquet was in progress when I entered. I was acclaimed with great delight, greeted boisterously by friends and introduced to such strangers as were there.

Entirely too weary to take much part in the revelry, I ate, drank quietly, listened to the toasts and songs, and studied the feasters.

Dom Vincente, of course, I knew, as I had been intimate with him for years; also his pretty niece, Ysabel, who was one reason I had accepted his invitation to come to that stinking wilderness. Her second cousin, Carlos, I knew and disliked—a sly, mincing fellow with a face like a mink's. Then there was my old friend, Luigi Verenza, an Italian; and his flirt of a sister, Marcita, making eyes at the men as usual. Then there was a short, stocky German who called himself Baron von Schiller; and Jean Desmarte, an out-at-the-elbows nobleman of Gascony; and Don Florenzo de Seville, a lean, dark, silent man, who called himself a Spaniard and wore a rapier nearly as long as himself.

There were others, men and women, but it was long ago and all their names and faces I do not remember.

But there was one man whose face somehow drew my gaze as an alchemist's magnet draws steel. He was a leanly built man of slightly more than medium height, dressed plainly, almost austerely, and he wore a sword almost as long as the Spaniard's.

But it was neither his clothes nor his sword which attracted my attention. It was his face. A refined, high-bred face, it was furrowed deep with lines that gave it

Wolfshead

a weary, haggard expression. Tiny scars flecked jaw and forehead as if torn by savage claws; I could have sworn the narrow gray eyes had a fleeting, haunted look in their expression at times.

I leaned over to that flirt, Marcita, and asked the name of the man, as it had slipt my mind that we had been introduced.

"De Montour, from Normandy," she answered. "A strange man. I don't think I like him."

"Then he resists your snares, my little enchantress?" I murmured, long friendship making me as immune from her anger as from her wiles. But she chose not to be angry and answered coyly, glancing from under demurely lowered lashes.

I watched de Montour much, feeling somehow a strange fascination. He ate lightly, drank much, seldom spoke, and then only to answer questions.

Presently, toasts making the rounds, I noticed his companions urging him to rise and give a health. At first he refused, then rose, upon their repeated urgings, and stood silent for a moment, goblet raised. He seemed to dominate, to overawe the group of revelers. Then with a mocking, savage laugh, he lifted the goblet above his head.

"To Solomon," he exclaimed, "who bound all devils! And thrice cursed be he for that some escaped!"

A toast and a curse in one! It was drunk silently, and with many sidelong, doubting glances.

That night I retired early, weary of the long sea voyage and my head spinning from the strength of the wine of which Dom Vincente kept such great stores.

My room was near the top of the castle and looked out toward the forests of the south and the river. The room was furnished in crude, barbaric splendor, as was all the rest of the castle.

Going to the window, I gazed out at the arquebusier pacing the castle grounds just inside the palisade; at the cleared space lying unsightly and barren in the moonlight; at the forest beyond; at the silent river.

Wolfshead

From the native quarters close to the river bank came the weird twanging of some rude lute, sounding a barbaric melody.

In the dark shadows of the forest some uncanny night-bird lifted a mocking voice. A thousand minor notes sounded—birds, and beasts, and the devil knows what else! Some great jungle cat began a hair-lifting yowling. I shrugged my shoulders and turned from the windows. Surely devils lurked in those somber depths.

There came a knock at my door and I opened it, to admit de Montour.

He strode to the window and gazed at the moon, which rode resplendent and glorious.

"The moon is almost full, is it not, Monsieur?" he remarked, turning to me. I nodded, and I could have sworn that he shuddered.

"Your pardon, Monsieur. I will not annoy you further." He turned to go, but at the door turned and retraced his steps.

"Monsieur," he almost whispered, with a fierce intensity, "whatever you do, be sure you bar and bolt your door tonight!"

Then he was gone, leaving me to stare after him bewilderedly.

I dozed off to sleep, the distant shouts of the revelers in my ears, and though I was weary, or perhaps because of it, I slept lightly. While I never really awoke until morning, sounds and noises seemed to drift to me through my veil of slumber, and once it seemed that something was prying and shoving against the bolted door.

As is to be supposed, most of the guests were in a beastly humor the following day and remained in their rooms most of the morning or else straggled down late. Besides Dom Vincente there were really only three of the masculine members sober: de Montour; the Spaniard, de Seville (as he called himself); and myself. The Spaniard never touched wine, and though de Montour consumed incredible quantities of it, it never affected him in any way.

Wolfshead

The ladies greeted us most graciously.

"S'truth, Signor," remarked that minx Marcita, giving me her hand with a gracious air that was like to make me snicker, "I am glad to see there are gentlemen among us who care more for our company than for the wine cup; for most of them are most surprizingly befuddled this morning."

Then with a most outrageous turning of her wondrous eyes, "Methinks someone was too drunk to be discreet last night—or not drunk enough. For unless my poor senses deceive me much, someone came fumbling at my door late in the night."

"Ha!" I exclaimed in quick anger, "some—!"

"No. Hush." She glanced about as if to see that we were alone, then: "Is it not strange that Signor de Montour, before he retired last night, instructed me to fasten my door firmly?"

"Strange," I murmured, but did not tell her that he had told me the same thing.

"And is it not strange, Pierre, that though Signor de Montour left the banquet hall even before you did, yet he has the appearance of one who has been up all night?"

I shrugged. A woman's fancies are often strange.

"Tonight," she said roguishly, "I will leave my door unbolted and see whom I catch."

"You will do no such thing."

She showed her little teeth in a contemptuous smile and displayed a small, wicked dagger.

"Listen, imp. De Montour gave me the same warning he did you. Whatever he knew, whoever prowled the halls last night, the object was more apt murder than amorous adventure. Keep you your doors bolted. The lady Ysabel shares your room, does she not?"

"Not she. And I send my woman to the slave quarters at night," she murmured, gazing mischievously at me from beneath drooping eyelids.

"One would think you a girl of no character from your talk," I told her, with the frankness of youth and of

Wolfshead

long friendship. "Walk with care, young lady, else I tell your brother to spank you."

And I walked away to pay my respects to Ysabel. The Portuguese girl was the very opposite of Marcita, being a shy, modest young thing, not so beautiful as the Italian, but exquisitely pretty in an appealing, almost childish air. I once had thoughts—Hi ho! To be young and foolish!

Your pardon, Messieurs. An old man's mind wanders. It was of de Montour that I meant to tell you—de Montour and Dom Vincente's mink-faced cousin.

A band of armed natives were thronged about the gates, kept at a distance by the Portuguese soldiers. Among them were some score of young men and women all naked, chained neck to neck. Slaves they were, captured by some warlike tribe and brought for sale. Dom Vincente looked them over personally.

Followed a long haggling and bartering, of which I quickly wearied and turned away, wondering that a man of Dom Vincente's rank could so demean himself as to stoop to trade.

But I strolled back when one of the natives of the village nearby came up and interrupted the sale with a long harangue to Dom Vincente.

While they talked de Montour came up, and presently Dom Vincente turned to us and said, "One of the woodcutters of the village was torn to pieces by a leopard or some such beast last night. A strong young man and unmarried."

"A leopard? Did they see it?" suddenly asked de Montour, and when Dom Vincente said no, that it came and went in the night, de Montour lifted a trembling hand and drew it across his forehead, as if to brush away cold sweat.

"Look you, Pierre," quoth Dom Vincente, "I have here a slave who, wonder of wonders, desires to be your man. Though the devil only knows why."

Wolfshead

He led up a slim young Jakri, a mere youth, whose main asset seemed a merry grin.

"He is yours," said Dom Vincente. "He is goodly trained and will make a fine servant. And look ye, a slave is of an advantage over a servant, for all he requires is food and a loincloth or so with a touch of the whip to keep him in his place."

It was not long before I learned why Gola wished to be "my man," choosing me among all the rest. It was because of my hair. Like many dandies of that day, I wore it long and curled, the strands falling to my shoulders. As it happened, I was the only man of the party who so wore my hair, and Gola would sit and gaze at it in silent admiration for hours at a time, or until, growing nervous under his unblinking scrutiny, I would boot him forth.

It was that night that a brooding animosity, hardly apparent, between Baron von Schiller and Jean Desmarte broke out into a flame.

As usual, woman was the cause. Marcita carried on a most outrageous flirtation with both of them.

That was not wise. Desmarte was a wild young fool. Von Schiller was a lustful beast. But when, Messieurs, did woman ever use wisdom?

Their hate flamed to a murderous fury when the German sought to kiss Marcita.

Swords were clashing in an instant. But before Dom Vincente could thunder a command to halt, Luigi was between the combatants, and had beaten their swords down, hurling them back viciously.

"Signori," said he softly, but with a fierce intensity, "is it the part of high-bred signori to fight over my sister? Ha, by the toenails of Satan, for the toss of a coin I would call you both out! You, Marcita, go to your chamber, instantly, nor leave until I give you permission."

And she went, for, independent though she was, none cared to face the slim, effeminate-appearing youth when a tigerish snarl curled his lips, a murderous gleam lightened his dark eyes.

Wolfshead

Apologies were made, but from the glances the two rivals threw at each other, we knew that the quarrel was not forgotten and would blaze forth again at the slightest pretext.

Late that night I woke suddenly with a strange, eery feeling of horror. Why, I could not say. I rose, saw that the door was firmly bolted, and seeing Gola asleep on the floor, kicked him awake irritably.

And just as he got up, hastily, rubbing himself, the silence was broken by a wild scream, a scream that rang through the castle and brought a startled shout from the arquebusier pacing the palisade; a scream from the mouth of a girl, frenzied with terror.

Gola squawked and dived behind the divan. I jerked the door open and raced down the dark corridor. Dashing down a winding stair, I caromed into someone at the bottom and we tumbled headlong.

He gasped something and I recognized the voice of Jean Desmarte. I hauled him to his feet, and raced along, he following; the screams had ceased, but the whole castle was in an uproar, voices shouting, the clank of weapons, lights flashing up, Dom Vincente's voice shouting for the soldiers, the noise of armed men rushing through the rooms and falling over each other. With all the confusion, Desmarte, the Spaniard, and I reached Marcita's room just as Luigi darted inside and snatched his sister into his arms.

Others rushed in, carrying lights and weapons, shouting, demanding to know what was occurring.

The girl lay quietly in her brother's arms, her dark hair loose and rippling over her shoulders, her dainty night-garments torn to shreds and exposing her lovely body. Long scratches showed upon her arms, breasts and shoulders.

Presently, she opened her eyes, shuddered, then shrieked wildly and clung frantically to Luigi, begging him not to let something take her.

"The door!" she whimpered. "I left it unbarred. And

something crept into my room through the darkness. I struck at it with my dagger and it hurled me to the floor, tearing, tearing at me. Then I fainted."

"Where is von Schiller?" asked the Spaniard, a fierce glint in his dark eyes. Every man glanced at his neighbor. All the guests were there except the German. I noted de Montour gazing at the terrified girl, his face more haggard than usual. And I thought it strange that he wore no weapon.

"Aye, von Schiller!" exclaimed Desmarte fiercely. And half of us followed Dom Vincente out into the corridor. We began a vengeful search through the castle, and in a small, dark hallway we found von Schiller. On his face he lay, in a crimson, ever-widening stain.

"This is the work of some native!" exclaimed Desmarte, face aghast.

"Nonsense," bellowed Dom Vincente. "No native from the outside could pass the soldiers. All slaves, von Schiller's among them, were barred and bolted in the slave quarters, except Gola, who sleeps in Pierre's room, and Ysabel's woman."

"But who else could have done this deed?" exclaimed Desmarte in a fury.

"You!" I said abruptly; "else why ran you so swiftly away from the room of Marcita?"

"Curse you, you lie!" he shouted, and his swift-drawn sword leaped for my breast; but quick as he was, the Spaniard was quicker. Desmarte's rapier clattered against the wall and Desmarte stood like a statue, the Spaniard's motionless point just touching his throat.

"Bind him," said the Spaniard without passion.

"Put down your blade, Don Florenzo," commanded Dom Vincente, striding forward and dominating the scene. "Signor Desmarte, you are one of my best friends, but I am the only law here and duty must be done. Give your word that you will not seek to escape."

"I give it," replied the Gascon calmly. "I acted hastily. I apologize. I was not intentionally running away,

Wolfshead

but the halls and corridors of this cursed castle confuse me."

Of us all, probably but one man believed him.

"Messieurs!" De Montour stepped forward. "This youth is not guilty. Turn the German over."

Two soldiers did as he asked. De Montour shuddered, pointing. The rest of us glanced once, then recoiled in horror.

"Could man have done that thing?"

"With a dagger—" began someone.

"No dagger makes wounds like that," said the Spaniard. "The German was torn to pieces by the talons of some frightful beast."

We glanced about us, half expecting some hideous monster to leap upon us from the shadows.

We searched that castle; every foot, every inch of it. And we found no trace of any beast.

Dawn was breaking when I returned to my room, to find that Gola had barred himself in; and it took me nearly a half-hour to convince him to let me in.

Having smacked him soundly and berated him for his cowardice, I told him what had taken place, as he could understand French and could speak a weird mixture which he proudly called French.

His mouth gaped and only the whites of his eyes showed as the tale reached its climax.

"Ju ju!" he whispered fearsomely. "Fetish man!"

Suddenly an idea came to me. I had heard vague tales, little more than hints of legends, of the devilish leopard cult that existed on the West Coast. No white man had ever seen one of its votaries, but Dom Vincente had told us tales of beast-men, disguised in skins of leopards, who stole through the midnight jungle and slew and devoured. A ghastly thrill traveled up and down my spine, and in an instant I had Gola in a grasp which made him yell.

"Was that a leopard-man?" I hissed, shaking him viciously.

Wolfshead

"Massa, massa!" he gasped. "Me good boy! Ju ju man get! More besser no tell!"

"You'll tell me!" I gritted, renewing my endeavors, until, his hands waving feeble protests, he promised to tell me what he knew.

"No leopard-man!" he whispered, and his eyes grew big with supernatural fear. "Moon, he full, woodcutter find, him heap clawed. Find 'nother woodcutter. Big Massa (Dom Vincente) say, 'leopard.' No leopard. But leopard-man, he come to kill. Something kill leopard-man! Heap claw! Hai, hai! Moon full again. Something come in lonely hut; claw um woman, claw um pick'nin. Man find um claw up. Big Massa say 'leopard.' Full moon again, and woodcutter find, heap clawed. Now come in castle. No leopard. But always footmarks of a man!"

I gave a startled, incredulous exclamation.

It was true, Gola averred. Always the footprints of a man led away from the scene of the murder. Then why did the natives not tell the Big Massa that he might hunt down the fiend? Here Gola assumed a crafty expression and whispered in my ear, The footprints were of a man who wore shoes!

Even assuming that Gola was lying, I felt a thrill of unexplainable horror. Who, then, did the natives believe was doing these frightful murders?

And he answered: Dom Vincente!

By this time, Messieurs, my mind was in a whirl.

What was the meaning of all this? Who slew the German and sought to ravish Marcita? And as I reviewed the crime, it appeared to me that murder rather than rape was the object of the attack.

Why did de Montour warn us, and then appear to have knowledge of the crime, telling us that Desmarte was innocent and then proving it?

It was all beyond me.

The tale of the slaughter got among the natives, in spite of all we could do, and they appeared restless and nervous, and thrice that day Dom Vincente had a black lashed for insolence. A brooding atmosphere pervaded the castle.

I considered going to Dom Vincente with Gola's tale, but decided to wait awhile.

The women kept to their chambers that day, the men were restless and moody. Dom Vincente announced that the sentries would be doubled and some would patrol the corridors of the castle itself. I found myself musing cynically that if Gola's suspicions were true, sentries would be of little good.

I am not, Messieurs, a man to brook such a situation with patience. And I was young then. So as we drank before retiring, I flung my goblet on the table and angrily announced that in spite of man, beast or devil, I slept that night with doors flung wide. And I tramped angrily to my chamber.

Again, as on the first night, de Montour came. And his face was as a man who has looked into the gaping gates of hell.

"I have come," he said, "to ask you—nay, Monsieur, to implore you—to reconsider your rash determination."

I shook my head impatiently.

"You are resolved? Yes? Then I ask you do to this for me, that after I enter my chamber, you will bolt my doors from the outside."

I did as he asked, and then made my way back to my chamber, my mind in a maze of wonderment. I had sent Gola to the slave quarters, and I laid rapier and dagger close at hand. Nor did I go to bed, but crouched in a great chair, in the darkness. Then I had much ado to keep from sleeping. To keep myself awake, I fell to musing on the strange words of de Montour. He seemed to be laboring under great excitement; his eyes hinted of ghastly mysteries known to him alone. And yet his face was not that of a wicked man.

Suddenly the notion took me to go to his chamber and talk with him.

Walking those dark passages was a shuddersome task, but eventually I stood before de Montour's door. I called softly. Silence. I reached out a hand and felt splintered fragments of wood. Hastily I struck flint and steel which I carried, and the flaming tinder showed the great oaken door sagging on its mighty hinges; showed a door smashed and splintered from the inside. And the chamber of de Montour was unoccupied.

Some instinct prompted me to hurry back to my room, swiftly but silently, shoeless feet treading softly. And as I neared the door, I was aware of something in the darkness before me. Something which crept in from a side corridor and glided stealthily along.

In a wild panic of fear I leaped, striking wildly and aimlessly in the darkness. My clenched fist encountered a human head, and something went down with a crash. Again I struck a light; a man lay senseless on the floor, and he was de Montour.

I thrust a candle into a niche in the wall, and just then de Montour's eyes opened and he rose uncertainly.

"You!" I exclaimed, hardly knowing what I said. "You, of all men!"

He merely nodded.

"You killed von Schiller?"

"Yes."

I recoiled with a gasp of horror.

"Listen." He raised his hand. "Take your rapier and run me through. No man will touch you."

"No," I exclaimed. "I can not."

"Then, quick," he said hurriedly, "get into your chamber and bolt the door. Haste! It will return!"

"What will return?" I asked, with a thrill of horror. "If it will harm me, it will harm you. Come into the chamber with me."

"No, no!" he fairly shrieked, springing back from my outstretched arm. "Haste, haste! It left me for an instant, but it will return." Then in a low-pitched voice of indescribable horror: "It is returning. It is here now!"

And I felt a something, a formless, shapeless presence near. A thing of frightfulness.

De Montour was standing, legs braced, arms

thrown back, fists clenched. The muscles bulged beneath his skin, his eyes widened and narrowed, the veins stood out upon his forehead as if in great physical effort. As I looked, to my horror, out of nothing, a shapeless, nameless something took vague form! Like a shadow it moved upon de Monteur.

It was hovering about him! Good God, it was merging, becoming one with the man!

De Montour swayed; a great gasp escaped him. The dim thing vanished. De Montour wavered. Then he turned toward me, and may God grant that I never look on a face like that again!

It was a hideous, a bestial face. The eyes gleamed with a frightful ferocity; the snarling lips were drawn back from gleaming teeth, which to my startled gaze appeared more like bestial fangs than human teeth.

Silently the thing (I can not call it a human) slunk toward me. Gasping with horror I sprang back and through the door, just as the thing launched itself through the air, with a sinuous motion which even then made me think of a leaping wolf. I slammed the door, holding it against the frightful thing which hurled itself again and again against it.

Finally it desisted and I heard it slink stealthily off down the corridor. Faint and exhausted I sat down, waiting, listening. Through the open window wafted the breeze, bearing all the scents of Africa, the spicy and the foul. From the native village came the sound of a native drum. Other drums answered farther up the river and back in the bush. Then from somewhere in the jungle, horridly incongruous, sounded the long, high-pitched call of a timber wolf. My soul revolted.

Dawn brought a tale of terrified villagers, of a Negro woman torn by some fiend of the night, barely escaping. And to de Montour I went.

On the way I met Dom Vincente. He was perplexed and angry.

"Some hellish thing is at work in this castle," he said. "Last night, though I have said naught of it to anyone,

Wolfshead

something leaped upon the back of one of the arquebusiers, tore the leather jerkin from his shoulders and pursued him to the barbican. More, someone locked de Montour into his room last night, and he was forced to smash the door to get out."

He strode on, muttering to himself, and I proceeded down the stairs, more puzzled than ever.

De Montour sat upon a stool, gazing out the window. An indescribable air of weariness was about him.

His long hair was uncombed and tousled, his garments were tattered. With a shudder I saw faint crimson stains upon his hands, and noted that the nails were torn and broken.

He looked up as I came in, and waved me to a seat. His face was worn and haggard, but was that of a man.

After a moment's silence, he spoke.

"I will tell you my strange tale. Never before has it passed my lips, and why I tell you, knowing that you will not believe me, I can not say."

And then I listened to what was surely the wildest, the most fantastic, the weirdest tale ever heard by man.

"Years ago," said de Montour, "I was upon a military mission in northern France. Alone, I was forced to pass through the fiend-haunted woodlands of Villefère. In those frightful forests I was beset by an inhuman, a ghastly thing—a werewolf. Beneath a midnight moon we fought, and slew it. Now this is the truth: that if a werewolf is slain in the half-form of a man, its ghost will haunt its slayer through eternity. But if it is slain as a wolf, hell gapes to receive it. The true werewolf is not (as many think) a man who may take the form of a wolf, but a wolf who takes the form of a man!

"Now listen, my friend, and I will tell you of the wisdom, the hellish knowledge that is mine, gained through many a frightful deed, imparted to me amid the ghastly shadows of midnight forests where fiends and half-beasts roamed.

"In the beginning, the world was strange, mis-

Wolfshead

shapen. Grotesque beasts wandered through its jungles. Driven from another world, ancient demons and fiends came in great numbers and settled upon this newer, younger world. Long the forces of good and evil warred.

"A strange beast, known as man, wandered among the other beasts, and since good or bad must have a concrete form ere either accomplishes its desire, the spirits of good entered man. The fiends entered other beasts, reptiles and birds; and long and fiercely waged the age-old battle. But man conquered. The great dragons and serpents were slain and with them the demons. Finally, Solomon, wise beyond the ken of man, made great war upon them, and by virtue of his wisdom, slew, seized and bound. But there were some which were the fiercest, the boldest, and though Solomon drove them out he could not conquer them. Those had taken the form of wolves. As the ages passed, wolf and demon became merged. No longer could the fiend leave the body of the wolf at will. In many instances, the savagery of the wolf overcame the subtlety of the demon and enslaved him, so the wolf became again only a beast, a fierce, cunning beast, but merely a beast. But of the werewolves, there are many, even yet.

And during the time of the full moon, the wolf may take the form, or the half-form of a man. When the moon hovers at her zenith, however, the wolf-spirit again takes ascendency and the werewolf becomes a true wolf once more. But if it is slain in the form of a man, then the spirit is free to haunt its slayer through the ages.

"Harken now. I had thought to have slain the thing after it had changed to its true shape. But I slew it an instant too soon. The moon, though it approached the zenith, had not yet reached it, nor had the thing taken on fully the wolf-form.

"Of this I knew nothing and went my way. But when the next time approached for the full moon, I began to be aware of a strange, malicious influence. An atmosphere of horror hovered in the air and I was aware of inexplicable, uncanny impulses.

Wolfshead

"One night in a small village in the center of a great forest, the influence came upon me with full power. It was night, and the moon, nearly full, was rising over the forest. And between the moon and me, I saw, floating in the upper air, ghostly and barely discernible, the outline of a wolf's head!

"I remember little of what happened thereafter. I remember, dimly, clambering into the silent street, remember struggling, resisting briefly, vainly, and the rest is a crimson maze, until I came to myself the next morning and found my garments and hands caked and stained crimson; and heard the horrified chattering of the villagers, telling of a pair of clandestine lovers, slaughtered in a ghastly manner, scarcely outside the village, torn to pieces as if by wild beasts, as if by wolves.

"From that village I fled aghast, but I fled not alone. In the day I could not feel the drive of my fearful captor, but when night fell and the moon rose, I ranged the silent forest, a frightful thing, a slayer of humans, a fiend in a man's body.

"God, the battles I have fought! But always it overcame me and drove me ravening after some new victim. But after the moon had passed its fullness, the thing's power over me ceased suddenly. Nor did it return until three nights before the moon was full again.

"Since then I have roamed the world—fleeing, fleeing, seeking to escape. Always the thing follows, taking possession of my body when the moon is full. Gods, the frightful deeds I have done!

"I would have slain myself long ago, but I dare not. For the soul of a suicide is accurst, and my soul would be forever hunted through the flames of hell. And harken, most frightful of all, my slain body would forever roam the earth, moved and inhabited by the soul of the werewolf! Can any thought be more ghastly?

"And I seem immune to the weapons of man. Swords have pierced me, daggers have hacked me. I am covered with scars. Yet never have they struck me down. In Germany they bound and led me to the block. There

Wolfshead

would I have willingly placed my head, but the thing came upon me, and breaking my bonds, I slew and fled. Up and down the world I have wandered, leaving horror and slaughter in my trail. Chains, cells, can not hold me. The thing is fastened to me through all eternity.

"In desperation I accepted Dom Vincente's invitation, for look you, none knows of my frightful double life, since no one could recognize me in the clutch of the demon; and few, seeing me, live to tell of it.

"My hands are red, my soul doomed to everlasting flames, my mind is torn with remorse for my crimes. And yet I can do nothing to help myself. Surely, Pierre, no man ever knew the hell that I have known.

"Yes, I slew von Schiller, and I sought to destroy the girl Marcita. Why I did not, I can not say, for I have slain both women and men.

"Now, if you will, take your sword and slay me, and with my last breath I will give you the good God's blessing. No?

"You know now my tale and you see before you a man, fiend-haunted for all eternity."

My mind was spinning with wonderment as I left the room of de Montour. What to do, I knew not. It seemed likely that he would yet murder us all, and yet I could not bring myself to tell Dom Vincente all. From the bottom of my soul I pitied de Montour.

So I kept my peace, and in the days that followed I made occasion to seek him out and converse with him. A real friendship sprang up between us.

About this time that black devil, Gola, began to wear an air of suppressed excitement, as if he knew something he wished desperately to tell, but would not or else dared not.

So the days passed in feasting, drinking and hunting, until one night de Montour came to my chamber and pointed silently at the moon which was just rising.

"Look ye," he said, "I have a plan. I will give it out that I am going into the jungle for hunting and will go forth, apparently for several days. But at night I will

Wolfshead

return to the castle, and you must lock me into the dungeon which is used as a storeroom."

This we did, and I managed to slip down twice a day and carry food and drink to my friend. He insisted on remaining in the dungeon even in the day, for though the fiend had never exerted its influence over him in the daytime, and he believed it powerless then, yet he would take no chances.

It was during this time that I began to notice that Dom Vincente's mink-faced cousin, Carlos, was forcing his attentions upon Ysabel, who was his second cousin, and who seemed to resent those attentions.

Myself, I would have challenged him for a duel for the toss of a coin, for I despised him, but it was really none of my affair. However, it seemed that Ysabel feared him.

My friend Luigi, by the way, had become enamored of the dainty Portuguese girl, and was making swift love to her daily.

And de Montour sat in his cell and reviewed his ghastly deeds until he battered the bars with his bare hands.

And Don Florenzo wandered about the castle grounds like a dour Mephistopheles.

And the other guests rode and quarreled and drank.

And Gola slithered about, eyeing me if always on the point of imparting momentous information. What wonder if my nerves became rasped to the shrieking point?

Each day the natives grew surlier and more and more sullen and intractable.

One night, not long before the full of the moon, I entered the dungeon where de Montour sat.

He looked up quickly.

"You dare much, coming to me in the night."

I shrugged my shoulders, seating myself.

A small barred window let in the night scents and sounds of Africa.

"Hark to the native drums," I said. "For the past week they have sounded almost incessantly."

De Montour assented.

Wolfshead

"The natives are restless. Methinks 'tis deviltry they are planning. Have you noticed that Carlos is much among them?"

"No," I answered, "but 'tis like there will be a break between him and Luigi. Luigi is paying court to Ysabel."

So we talked, when suddenly de Montour became silent and moody, answering only in monosyllables.

The moon rose and peered in at the barred windows. De Montour's face was illuminated by its beams.

And then the hand of horror grasped me. On the wall behind de Montour appeared a shadow, a shadow clearly defined of a wolf's head!

At the same instant de Montour felt its influence. With a shriek he bounded from his stool.

He pointed fiercely, and as with trembling hands I slammed and bolted the door behind me, I felt him hurl his weight against it. As I fled up the stairway I heard a wild raving and battering at the iron-bound door. But with all the werewolf's might the great door held.

As I entered my room, Gola dashed in and gasped out the tale he had been keeping for days.

I listened, incredulously, and then dashed forth to find Dom Vincente.

I was told that Carlos had asked him to accompany him to the village to arrange a sale of slaves.

My informer was Don Florenzo of Seville, and when I gave him a brief outline of Gola's tale, he accompanied me.

Together we dashed through the castle gate, flinging a word to the guards, and down the landing toward the village.

Dom Vincente, Dom Vincente, walk with care, keep sword loosened in its sheath! Fool, fool, to walk in the night with Carlos, the traitor!

They were nearing the village when we caught up with them. "Dom Vincente!" I exclaimed; "return instantly to the castle. Carlos is selling you into the hands of the natives! Gola has told me that he lusts for your wealth and for Ysabel! A terrified native babbled to him of booted footprints near the places where the woodcut-

Wolfshead

ters were murdered, and Carlos has made the blacks believe that the slayer was you! Tonight the natives were to rise and slay every man in the castle except Carlos! Do you not believe me, Dom Vincente?"

"Is this the truth, Carlos?" asked Dom Vincente, in amaze.

Carlos laughed mockingly.

"The fool speaks truth," he said, "but it accomplishes you nothing. Ho!"

He shouted as he leaped for Dom Vincente. Steel flashed in the moonlight and the Spaniard's sword was through Carlos ere he could move.

And the shadows rose about us. Then it was back to back, sword and dagger, three men against a hundred. Spears flashed, and a fiendish yell went up from savage throats. I spitted three natives in as many thrusts and then went down from a stunning swing from a war-club, and an instant later Dom Vincente fell upon me, with a spear in one arm and another through the leg. Don Florenzo was standing above us, sword leaping like a live thing, when a charge of the arquebusiers swept the river bank clear and we were borne into the castle.

The black hordes came with a rush, spears flashing like a wave of steel, a thunderous roar of savagery going up to the skies.

Time and again they swept up the slopes, bounding the moat, until they were swarming over the palisades. And time and again the fire of the hundred-odd defenders hurled them back.

They had set fire to the plundered warehouses, and their light vied with the light of the moon. Just across the river there was a larger storehouse, and about this hordes of the natives gathered, tearing it apart for plunder.

"Would that they would drop a torch upon it," said Dom Vincente, "for naught is stored therein save some thousand pounds of gunpowder. I dared not store the treacherous stuff this side of the river. All the tribes of the river and coast have gathered for our slaughter and all my ships are upon the seas. We may hold out awhile, but eventually they will swarm the palisade and put us to the slaughter."

I hastened to the dungeon wherein de Montour sat. Outside the door I called to him and he bade me enter in voice which told me the fiend had left him for an instant.

"The blacks have risen," I told him.

"I guessed as much. How goes the battle?"

I gave him the details of the betrayal and the fight, and mentioned the powder-house across the river. He sprang to his feet.

"Now by my hag-ridden soul!" he exclaimed. "I will fling the dice once more with hell! Swift, let me out of the castle! I will essay to swim the river and set off yon powder!"

"It is insanity!" I exclaimed. "A thousand blacks lurk between the palisades and the river, and thrice that number beyond! The river itself swarms with crocodiles!"

"I will attempt it!" he answered, a great light in his face. "If I can reach it, some thousand natives will lighten the siege; if I am slain, then my soul is free and mayhap will gain some forgiveness for that I gave my life to atone for my crimes."

Then, "Haste," he exclaimed, "for the demon is returning! Already I feel his influence! Haste ye!"

For the castle gates we sped, and as de Montour ran he gasped as a man in a terrific battle.

At the gate he pitched headlong, then rose, to spring through it. Wild yells greeted him from the natives.

The arquebusiers shouted curses at him and at me. Peering down from the top of the palisades I saw him turn from side to side uncertainly. A score of natives were rushing recklessly forward, spears raised.

Then the eery wolf-yell rose to the skies, and de Montour bounded forward. Aghast, the natives paused, and before a man of them could move he was among them. Wild shrieks, not of rage, but of terror.

In amazement the arquebusiers held their fire.

Wolfshead

Straight through the group of blacks de Montour charged, and when they broke and fled, three of them fled not.

A dozen steps de Montour took in pursuit; then stopped stock-still. A moment he stood so, while spears flew about him, then turned and ran swiftly in the direction of the river.

A few steps from the river another band of blacks barred his way. In the flaming light of the burning houses the scene was clearly illuminated. A thrown spear tore through de Montour's shoulder. Without pausing in his stride he tore it forth and drove it through a native, leaping over his body to get among the others.

They could not face the fiend-driven white man. With shrieks they fled, and de Montour, bounding upon the back of one, brought him down.

Then he rose, staggered and sprang to the river bank. An instant he paused there and then vanished in the shadows.

"Name of the devil!" gasped Dom Vincente at my shoulder. "What manner of man is that? Was that de Montour?"

I nodded. The wild yells of the natives rose above the crackle of the arquebus fire. They were massed thick about the great warehouse across the river.

"They plan a great rush," said Dom Vincente. "They will swarm clear over the palisade, methinks. Ha!"

A crash that seemed to rip the skies apart! A burst of flame that mounted to the stars! The castle rocked with the explosion. Then silence, as the smoke, drifting away, showed only a great crater where the warehouse had stood.

I could tell of how Dom Vincente led a charge, crippled as he was, out of the castle gate and down the slope, to fall upon the terrified blacks who had escaped the explosion. I could tell of the slaughter, of the victory and the pursuit of the fleeing natives.

I could tell, too, Messieurs, of how I became separated from the band and of how I wandered far into

Wolfshead

the jungle, unable to find my way back to the coast.

I could tell how I was captured by a wandering band of slave raiders, and of how I escaped. But such is not my intention. In itself it would make a long tale; and it is of de Montour that I am speaking.

I thought much of the things that had passed and wondered if indeed de Montour reached the storehouse to blow it to the skies or whether it was but the deed of chance.

That a man could swim that reptile-swarming river, fiend-driven though he was, seemed impossible. And if he blew up the storehouse, he must have gone up with it.

So one night I pushed my way wearily through the jungle and sighted the coast, and close to the shore a small, tumbledown hut of thatch. To it I went, thinking to sleep therein if insects and reptiles would allow.

I entered the doorway and then stopped short. Upon a makeshift stool sat a man. He looked up as I entered and the rays of the moon fell across his face.

I started back with a ghastly thrill of horror. *It was de Montour, and the moon was full!*

Then as I stood, unable to flee, he rose and came toward me. And his face, though haggard as of a man who has looked into hell, was the face of a sane man.

"Come in, my friend," he said, and there was a great peace in his voice. "Come in and fear me not. The fiend has left me forever."

"But tell me, how conquered you?" I exclaimed as I grasped his hand.

"I fought a frightful battle, as I ran to the river," he answered, "for the fiend had me in its grasp and drove me to fall upon the natives. But for the first time my soul and mind gained ascendency for an instant, an instant just long enough to hold me to my purpose. And I believe the good saints came to my aid, for I was giving my life to save life.

"I leaped into the river and swam, and in an instant the crocodiles were swarming about me.

"Again in the clutch of the fiend I fought them, there

Wolfshead

in the river. Then suddenly the *thing* left me.

"I climbed from the river and fired the warehouse. The explosion hurled me hundreds of feet, and for days I wandered witless through the jungle.

"But the full moon came, and came again, and I felt not the influence of the fiend.

"I am free, free!" And a wondrous note of exultation, nay, *exaltation*, thrilled his words:

"My soul is free. Incredible as it seems, the demon lies drowned upon the bed of the river, or else inhabits the body of one of the savage reptiles that swim the ways of the Niger."

The Fire of Asshurbanipal

Yar Ali squinted carefully down the blue barrel of his Lee-Enfield, called devoutly on Allah and sent a bullet through the brain of a flying rider.

"*Allaho akbar!*"

The big Afghan shouted in glee, waving his weapon above his head, "God is great! By Allah, *sahib*, I have sent another one of the dogs to Hell!"

His companion peered cautiously over the rim of the sand-pit they had scooped with their hands. He was a lean and wiry American, Steve Clarney by name.

"Good work, old horse," said this person. "Four left. Look—they're drawing off."

The white-robed horsemen were indeed reining away, clustering together just out of accurate rifle-range, as if in council. There had been seven when they had first swooped down on the comrades, but the fire from the two rifles in the sand-pit had been deadly.

"Look, *sahib*—they abandon the fray!"

Yar Ali stood up boldly and shouted taunts at the departing riders, one of whom whirled and sent a bullet that kicked up sand thirty feet in front of the pit.

"They shoot like the sons of dogs," said Yar Ali in

The Fire of Asshurbanipal

complacent self-esteem. "By Allah, did you see that rogue plunge from his saddle as my lead went home? Up, *sahib*; let us run after them and cut them down!"

Paying no attention to this outrageous proposal—for he knew it was but one of the gestures Afghan nature continually demands—Steve rose, dusted off his breeches and gazing after the riders, now white specks far out on the desert, said musingly: "Those fellows ride as if they had some set purpose in mind—not a bit like men running from a licking."

"Aye," agreed Yar Ali promptly and seeing nothing inconsistent with his present attitude and recent bloodthirsty suggestion, "they ride after more of their kind—they are hawks who give up their prey not quickly. We had best move our position quickly, Steve *sahib*. They will come back—maybe in a few hours, maybe in a few days—it all depends on how far away lies the oasis of their tribe. But they will be back. We have guns and lives—they want both. And behold."

The Afghan levered out the empty shell and slipped a single cartridge into the breech of his rifle.

"My last bullet, *sahib*."

Steve nodded. "I've got three left."

The raiders whom their bullets had knocked from the saddle had been looted by their own comrades. No use searching the bodies which lay in the sand for ammunition. Steve lifted his canteen and shook it. Not much water remained. He knew that Yar Ali had only a little more than he, though the big Afridi, bred in a barren land, had used and needed less water than did the American; although the latter, judged from a white man's standards, was hard and tough as a wolf. As Steve unscrewed the canteen cap and drank very sparingly, he mentally reviewed the chain of events that had led them to their present position.

Wanderers, soldiers of fortune, thrown together by chance and attracted to each other by mutual admiration, he and Yar Ali had wandered from India up through Turkistan and down through Persia, an oddly assorted

The Fire of Asshurbanipal

but highly capable pair. Driven by the restless urge of inherent wanderlust, their avowed purpose—which they swore to and sometimes believed themselves—was the accumulation of some vague and undiscovered treasure, some pot of gold at the foot of some yet unborn rainbow.

Then in ancient Shiraz they had heard of the Fire of Asshurbanipal. From the lips of an ancient Persian trader, who only half believed what he repeated to them, they heard the tale that he in turn had heard from the babbling lips of delirium, in his distant youth. He had been a member of a caravan, fifty years before, which, wandering far on the southern shore of the Persian Gulf trading for pearls, had followed the tale of a rare pearl far into the desert.

The pearl, rumored found by a diver and stolen by a shaykh of the interior, they did not find, but they did pick up a Turk who was dying of starvation, thirst and a bullet wound in the thigh. As he died in delirium, he babbled a wild tale of a silent dead city of black stone set in the drifting sands of the desert far to the westward, and of a flaming gem clutched in the bony fingers of a skeleton on an ancient throne.

He had not dared bring it away with him, because of an overpowering brooding horror that haunted the place, and thirst had driven him into the desert again, where Bedouins had pursued and wounded him. Yet he had escaped, riding hard until his horse fell under him. He died without telling how he had reached the mythical city in the first place, but the old trader thought he must have come from the northwest—a deserter from the Turkish army, making a desperate attempt to reach the Gulf.

The men of the caravan had made no attempt to plunge still further into the desert in search of the city; for, said the old trader, they believed it to be the ancient, ancient City of Evil spoken of in the *Necronomicon* of the mad Arab Alhazred—the city of the dead on which an ancient curse rested. Legends named it vaguely: the Arabs called it *Beled-el-Djinn*, the City of Devils, and the Turks, *Kara-Shehr*, the Black City. And the gem was that an-

The Fire of Asshurbanipal

cient and accursed jewel belonging to a king of long ago, whom the Grecians called Sardanapalus and the Semitic peoples Asshurbanipal.

Steve had been fascinated by the tale. Admitting to himself that it was doubtless one of the ten thousand cock-and-bull myths booted about the East, still there was a possibility that he and Yar Ali had stumbled onto a trace of that pot of rainbow gold for which they searched. And Yar Ali had heard hints before of a silent city of the sands; tales had followed the eastbound caravans over the high Persian uplands and across the sands of Turkistan, into the mountain country and beyond—vague tales, whispers of a black city of the djinn, deep in the hazes of a haunted desert.

So, following the trail of the legend, the companions had come from Shiraz to a village on the Arabian shore of the Persian Gulf, and there had heard more from an old man who had been a pearl-driver in his youth. The loquacity of age was on him and he told tales repeated to him by wandering tribesmen who had them in turn from the wild nomads of the deep interior; and again Steve and Yar Ali heard of the still black city with giant beasts carved of stone, and the skeleton sultan who held the blazing gem.

And so, mentally swearing at himself for a fool, Steve had made the plunge, and Yar Ali, secure in the knowledge that all things lay on the lap of Allah, had come with him. Their scanty supply of money had been just sufficient to provide riding-camels and provisions for a bold flying invasion of the unknown. Their only chart had been the vague rumors that placed the supposed location of Kara-Shehr.

There had been days of hard travel, pushing the beasts and conserving water and food. Then, deep in the desert they invaded, they had encountered a blinding sand-wind in which they had lost the camels. After that came long miles of staggering through the sands, battered by a flaming sun, subsisting on rapidly dwindling water

The Fire of Asshurbanipal

from their canteens, and food Yar Ali had in a pouch. No thought of finding the mythical city now. They pushed on blindly, in hope of stumbling upon a spring; they knew that behind them no oases lay within a distance they could hope to cover on foot. It was a desperate chance, but their only one.

Then white-clad hawks had swooped down on them, out of the haze of the skyline, and from a shallow and hastily scooped trench the adventurers had exchanged shots with the wild riders who circled them at top speed. The bullets of the Bedouins had skipped through their makeshift fortifications, knocking dust into their eyes and flicking bits of cloth from their garments, but by good chance neither had been hit.

Their one bit of luck, reflected Clarney, as he cursed himself for a fool. What a mad venture it had been, anyway! To think that two men could so dare the desert and live, much less wrest from its abysmal bosom the secrets of the ages! And that crazy tale of a skeleton hand gripping a flaming jewel in a dead city—bosh! What utter rot! He must have been crazy himself to credit it, the American decided with the clarity of view that suffering and danger bring.

"Well, old horse," said Steve, lifting his rifle, "let's get going. It's a toss-up if we die of thirst or get sniped off by the desert-brothers. Anyway, we're doin' no good here."

"God gives," agreed Yar Ali cheerfully. "The sun sinks westward. Soon the coolness of night will be upon us. Perhaps we shall find water yet, *sahib*. Look, the terrain changes to the south."

Clarney shaded his eyes against the dying sun. Beyond a level, barren expanse of several miles width, the land did indeed become more broken; aborted hills were in evidence. The American slung his rifle over his arm and sighed.

"Heave ahead; we're food for the buzzards anyhow."

The Fire of Asshurbanipal

The sun sank and the moon rose, flooding the desert with weird silver light. Drifted sand glimmered in long ripples, as if a sea had suddenly been frozen into immobility. Steve, parched fiercely by a thirst he dared not fully quench, cursed beneath his breath. The desert was beautiful beneath the moon, with the beauty of a cold marble lorelei to lure men to destruction. What a mad quest! his weary brain reiterated; the Fire of Asshurbanipal retreated into the mazes of unreality with each dragging step. The desert became not merely a material wasteland, but the gray mists of the lost eons, in whose depths dreamed sunken things.

Clarney stumbled and swore; was he failing already? Yar Ali swung along with the easy, tireless stride of the mountain man, and Steve set his teeth, nerving himself to greater effort. They were entering the broken country at last, and the going became harder. Shallow gullies and narrow ravines knifed the earth with wavering patterns. Most of them were nearly filled with sand, and there was no trace of water.

"This country was once oasis country," commented Yar Ali. "Allah knows how many centuries ago the sand took it, as the sand has taken so many cities in Turkistan."

They swung on like dead men in a gray land of death. The moon grew red and sinister as she sank, and shadowy darkness settled over the desert before they had reached a point where they could see what lay beyond the broken belt. Even the big Afghan's feet began to drag, and Steve kept himself erect only by a savage effort of will. At last they toiled up a sort of ridge, on the southern side of which the land sloped downward.

"We rest," declared Steve. "There's no water in this hellish country. No use in goin' on for ever. My legs are stiff as gun-barrels. I couldn't take another step to save my neck. Here's a kind of stunted cliff, about as high as a man's shoulder, facing south. We'll sleep in the lee of it."

"And shall we not keep watch, Steve *sahib*?"

"We don't," answered Steve. "If the Arabs cut our

The Fire of Asshurbanipal

throats while we're asleep, so much the better. We're goners anyhow."

With which optimistic observation Clarney lay down stiffly in the deep sand. But Yar Ali stood, leaning forward, straining his eyes into the elusive darkness that turned the star-flecked horizons to murky wells of shadow.

"Something lies on the skyline to the south," he muttered uneasily. "A hill? I cannot tell, or even be sure that I see anything at all."

"You're seeing mirages already," said Steve irritably. "Lie down and sleep."

And so saying Steve slumbered.

The sun in his eyes awoke him. He sat up, yawning, and his first sensation was that of thirst. He lifted his canteen and wet his lips. One drink left. Yar Ali still slept. Steve's eyes wandered over the southern horizon and he started. He kicked the recumbent Afghan.

"Hey, wake up, Ali. I reckon you weren't seeing things after all. There's your hill—and a queer-lookin' one, too."

The Afridi woke as a wild thing wakes, instantly and completely, his hand leaping to his long knife as he glared about for enemies. His gaze followed Steve's pointing fingers and his eyes widened.

"By Allah and by Allah!" he swore. "We have come into a land of djinn! That is no hill—it is a city of stone in the midst of the sands!"

Steve bounded to his feet like a steel spring released. As he gazed with bated breath, a fierce shout escaped his lips. At his feet the slope of the ridge ran down into a wide and level expanse of sand that stretched away southward. And far away, across those sands, to his straining sight the "hill" slowly took shape, like a mirage growing from the drifting sands.

He saw great uneven walls, massive battlements; all about crawled the sands like a living, sensate thing, drifted high about the walls, softening the rugged

The Fire of Asshurbanipal

outlines. No wonder that at first glance the whole had appeared like a hill.

"Kara-Shehr!" Clarney exclaimed fiercely. "Beled-el-Djinn! The city of the dead! It wasn't a pipe-dream after all! We've found it—by Heaven, we've found it! Come on! Let's go!"

Yar Ali shook his head uncertainly and muttered something about evil djinn under his breath, but he followed. The sight of the ruins had swept from Steve his thirst and hunger, and the fatigue that a few hours' sleep had not fully overcome. He trudged on swiftly, oblivious to the rising heat, his eyes gleaming with the lust of the explorer. It was not altogether greed for the fabled gem that had prompted Steve Clarney to risk his life in that grim wilderness; deep in his soul lurked the age-old heritage of the white man, the urge to seek out the hidden places of the world, and that urge had been stirred to the depths by the ancient tales.

Now as they crossed the level wastes that separated the broken land from the city, they saw the shattered walls take clearer form and shape, as if they grew out of the morning sky. The city seemed built of huge blocks of black stone, but how high the walls had been there was no telling because of the sand that drifted high about their base; in many places they had fallen away and the sand hid the fragments entirely.

The sun reached her zenith and thirst intruded itself in spite of zeal and enthusiasm, but Steve fiercely mastered his suffering. His lips were parched and swollen, but he would not take that last drink until he had reached the ruined city. Yar Ali wet his lips from his own canteen and tried to share the remainder with his friend. Steve shook his head and plodded on.

In the ferocious heat of the desert afternoon they reached the ruin, and passing through a wide breach in the crumbling wall, gazed on the dead city. Sand choked the ancient streets and lent fantastic form to huge, fallen and half-hidden columns. So crumbled into decay and so

The Fire of Asshurbanipal

covered with sand was the whole that the explorers could make out little of the original plan of the city; now it was but a waste of drifted sand and crumbling stone over which brooded, like an invisible cloud, an aura of unspeakable antiquity.

But directly in front of them ran a broad avenue, the outline of which not even the ravaging sands and winds of time had been able to efface. On either side of the wide way were ranged huge columns, not unusually tall, even allowing for the sand that hid their bases, but incredibly massive. On the top of each column stood a figure carved from solid stone—great, somber images, half human, half bestial, partaking of the brooding brutishness of the whole city. Steve cried out in amazement.

"The winged bulls of Nineveh! The bulls with men's heads! By the saints, Ali, the old tales are true! The Assyrians did build this city! The whole tale's true! They must have come here when the Babylonians destroyed Assyria—why, this scene's a dead ringer for pictures I've seen—reconstructed scenes of Old Nineveh! And look!"

He pointed down the broad street to the great building which reared at the other end, a colossal, brooding edifice whose columns and walls of solid black stone blocks defied the winds and sands of time. The drifting, obliterating sea washed about its foundations, overflowing into its doorways, but it would require a thousand years to inundate the whole structure.

"An abode of devils!" muttered Yar Ali, uneasily.

"The temple of Baal!" exclaimed Steve. "Come on! I was afraid we'd find all the palaces and temples hidden by the sand and have to dig for the gem."

"Little good it will do us," muttered Yar Ali. "Here we die."

"I reckon so." Steve unscrewed the cap of his canteen. "Let's take our last drink. Anyway, we're safe from the Arabs. They'd never dare come here, with their superstitions. We'll drink and then we'll die, I reckon, but first we'll find the jewel. When I pass out, I want to have it in my hand. Maybe a few centuries later some lucky

The Fire of Asshurbanipal

son-of-a-gun will find our skeletons—and the gem. Here's to him, whoever he is!"

With which grim jest Clarney drained his canteen and Yar Ali followed suit. They had played their last ace; the rest lay on the lap of Allah.

They strode up the broad way, and Yar Ali, utterly fearless in the face of human foes, glanced nervously to right and left, half expecting to see a horned and fantastic face leering at him from behind a column. Steve himself felt the somber antiquity of the place, and almost found himself fearing a rush of bronze war chariots down the forgotten streets, or to hear the sudden menacing flare of bronze trumpets. The silence in dead cities was so much more intense, he reflected, than that on the open desert.

They came to the portals of the great temple. Rows of immense columns flanked the wide doorway, which was ankle-deep in sand, and from which sagged massive bronze frameworks that had once braced mighty doors, whose polished woodwork had rotted away centuries ago. They passed into a mighty hall of misty twilight, whose shadowy stone roof was upheld by columns like the trunks of forest trees. The whole effect of the architecture was one of awesome magnitude and sullen, breathtaking splendor, like a temple built by somber giants for the abode of dark gods.

Yar Ali walked fearfully, as if he expected to awake sleeping gods, and Steve, without the Afridi's superstitions, yet felt the gloomy majesty of the place lay somber hands on his soul.

No trace of a footprint showed in the deep dust on the floor; half a century had passed since the affrighted and devil-ridden Turk had fled these silent halls. As for the Bedouins, it was easy to see why those superstitious sons of the desert shunned this haunted city—and haunted it was, not by actual ghosts, perhaps, but by the shadows of lost splendors.

As they trod the sands of the hall, which seemed endless, Steve pondered many questions: How did these

The Fire of Asshurbanipal

fugitives from the wrath of frenzied rebels build this city? How did they pass through the country of their foes,—for Babylonia lay between Assyria and the Arabian desert. Yet there had been no other place for them to go; westward lay Syria and the sea, and north and east swarmed the "dangerous Medes," those fierce Aryans whose aid had stiffened the arm of Babylon to smite her foe to the dust.

Possibly, thought Steve, Kara-Shehr—whatever its name had been in those dim days—had been built as an outpost border city before the fall of the Assyrian empire, whither survivals of that overthrow fled. At any rate it was possible that Kara-Shehr had outlasted Nineveh by some centuries—a strange, hermit city, no doubt, cut off from the rest of the world.

Surely, as Yar Ali had said, this was once fertile country, watered by oases; and doubtless in the broken country they had passed over the night before, there had been quarries that furnished the stone for the building of the city.

Then what caused its downfall? Did the encroachment of the sands and the filling up of the springs cause the people to abandon it, or was Kara-Shehr a city of silence before the sands crept over the walls? Did the downfall come from within or without? Did civil war blot out the inhabitants, or were they slaughtered by some powerful foe from the desert? Clarney shook his head in baffled chagrin. The answers to those questions were lost in the maze of forgotten ages.

"Allaho akbar!" They had traversed the great shadowy hall and at its further end they came upon a hideous black stone altar, behind which loomed an ancient god, bestial and horrific. Steve shrugged his shoulders as he recognized the monstrous aspect of the image—aye, that was Baal, on which black altar in other ages many a screaming, writhing, naked victim had offered up its naked soul. The idol embodied in its utter, abysmal and sullen bestiality the whole soul of this demoniac city. Surely, thought Steve, the builders of

The Fire of Asshurbanipal

Nineveh and Kara-Shehr were cast in another mold from the people of today. Their art and culture were too ponderous, too grimly barren of the lighter aspects of humanity, to be wholly human, as modern man understands humanity. Their architecture was repellent; of high skill, yet so massive, sullen and brutish in effect as to be almost beyond the comprehension of moderns.

The adventurers passed through a narrow door which opened in the end of the hall close to the idol, and came into a series of wide, dim, dusty chambers connected by column-flanked corridors. Along these they strode in the gray ghostly light, and came at last to a wide stair, whose massive stone steps led upward and vanished in the gloom. Here Yar Ali halted.

"We have dared much, *sahib*," he muttered. "Is it wise to dare more?"

Steve, aquiver with eagerness, yet understood the Afghan's mind. "You mean we shouldn't go up those stairs?"

"They have an evil look. To what chambers of silence and horror may they lead? When djinn haunt deserted buildings, they lurk in the upper chambers. At any moment a demon may bite off our heads."

"We're dead men anyhow," grunted Steve. "But I tell you—you go on back through the hall and watch for the Arabs while I go upstairs."

"Watch for a wind on the horizon," responded the Afghan gloomily, shifting his rifle and loosening his long knife in its scabbard. "No Bedouin comes here. Lead on, *sahib*. Thou'rt mad after the manner of all Franks, but I would not leave thee to face the djinn alone."

So the companions mounted the massive stairs, their feet sinking deep into the accumulated dust of centuries at each step. Up and up they went, to an incredible height until the depths below merged into a vague gloom.

"We walk blind to our doom, *sahib*," muttered Yar Ali. "*Allah il allah*—and Muhammad is his Prophet! Nevertheless, I feel the presence of slumbering Evil and

The Fire of Asshurbanipal

never again shall I hear the wind blowing up the Khyber Pass."

Steve made no reply. He did not like the breathless silence that brooded over the ancient temple, nor the grisly gray light that filtered from some hidden source.

Now above them the gloom lightened somewhat and they emerged into a vast circular chamber, grayly illumined by light that filtered in through the high, pierced ceiling. But another radiance lent itself to the illumination. A cry burst from Steve's lips, echoed by Yar Ali.

Standing on the top step of the broad stone stair, they looked directly across the broad chamber, with its dust-covered heavy tile floor and bare black stone walls. From above the center of the chamber, massive steps led up to a stone dais, and on this dais stood a marble throne. About this throne glowed and shimmered an uncanny light, and the awe-struck adventurers gasped as they saw its source. On the throne slumped a human skeleton, an almost shapeless mass of moldering bones. A fleshless hand sagged outstretched upon the broad marble throne-arm, and in its grisly clasp there pulsed and throbbed like a living thing, a great crimson stone.

The Fire of Asshurbanipal! Even after they had found the lost city Steve had not really allowed himself to believe that they would find the gem, or that it even existed in reality. Yet he could not doubt the evidence of his eyes, dazzled by that evil, incredible glow. With a fierce shout he sprang across the chamber and up the steps. Yar Ali was at his heels, but when Steve would have seized the gem, the Afghan laid a hand on his arm.

"Wait!" exclaimed the big Muhammadan. "Touch it not yet, *sahib!* A curse lies on ancient things—and surely this is a thing triply accursed! Else why has it lain here untouched in a country of thieves for so many centuries? It is not well to disturb the possessions of the dead."

"Bosh!" snorted the American. "Superstitions! The

The Fire of Asshurbanipal

Bedouins were scared by the tales that have come down to 'em from their ancestors. Being desert-dwellers they mistrust cities anyway, and no doubt this one had an evil reputation in its lifetime. And nobody except Bedouins have seen this place before, except that Turk, who was probably half demented with suffering.

"These bones may be those of the king mentioned in the legend—the dry desert air preserves such things indefinitely—but I doubt it. May be Assyrian—most likely Arab—some beggar that got the gem and then died on that throne for some reason or other."

The Afghan scarcely heard him. He was gazing in fearful fascination at the great stone, as a hypnotized bird stares into a serpent's eye.

"Look at it, *sahib!*" he whispered. "What is it? No such gem as this was ever cut by mortal hands! Look how it throbs and pulses like the heart of a cobra!"

Steve was looking, and he was aware of a strange undefined feeling of uneasiness. Well versed in the knowledge of precious stones, he had never seen a stone like this. At first glance he had supposed it to be a monster ruby, as told in the legends. Now he was not sure, and he had a nervous feeling that Yar Ali was right, that this was no natural, normal gem. He could not classify the style in which it was cut, and such was the power of its lurid radiance that he found it difficult to gaze at it closely for any length of time. The whole setting was not one calculated to soothe restless nerves. The deep dust on the floor suggested an unwholesome antiquity; the gray light evoked a sense of unreality, and the heavy black walls towered grimly, hinting at hidden things.

"Let's take the stone and go!" muttered Steve, an unaccustomed panicky dread rising in his bosom.

"Wait!" Yar Ali's eyes were blazing, and he gazed, not at the gem, but at the sullen stone walls. "We are flies in the lair of the spider! *Sahib*, as Allah lives, it is more than the ghosts of old fears that lurk over this city of horror! I feel the presence of peril, as I have felt it

The Fire of Asshurbanipal

before—as I felt it in a jungle cavern where a python lurked unseen in the darkness—as I felt it in the temple of Thuggee where the hidden stranglers of Siva crouched to spring upon us—as I feel it now, tenfold!"

Steve's hair prickled. He knew that Yar Ali was a grim veteran, not to be stampeded by silly fear or senseless panic; he well remembered the incidents referred to by the Afghan, as he remembered other occasions upon which Yar Ali's Oriental telepathic instinct had warned him of danger before that danger was seen or heard.

"What is it, Yar Ali?" he whispered.

The Afghan shook his head, his eyes filled with a weird mysterious light as he listened to the dim occult promptings of his subconsciousness.

"I know not; I know it is close to us, and that it is very ancient and very evil. I think——" Suddenly he halted and wheeled, the eery light vanishing from his eyes to be replaced by a glare of wolf-like fear and suspicion.

"Hark, *sahib!*" he snapped. "Ghosts or dead men mount the stair!"

Steve stiffened as the stealthy pad of soft sandals on stone reached his ear.

"By Judas, Ali!" he rapped; "something's out there——"

The ancient walls re-echoed to a chorus of wild yells as a horde of savage figures flooded the chamber. For one dazed insane instant Steve believed wildly that they were being attacked by re-embodied warriors of a vanished age; then the spiteful crack of a bullet past his ear and the acrid smell of powder told him that their foes were material enough. Clarney cursed; in their fancied security they had been caught like rats in a trap by the pursuing Arabs.

Even as the American threw up his rifle, Yar Ali fired point-blank from the hip with deadly effect, hurled his empty rifle into the horde and went down the steps like a hurricane, his three-foot Khyber knife shimmering in his hairy hand. Into his gusto for battle went real relief

The Fire of Asshurbanipal

that his foes were human. A bullet ripped the turban from his head, but an Arab went down with a split skull beneath the hillman's first, shearing stroke.

A tall Bedouin clapped his gun-muzzle to the Afghan's side, but before he could pull the trigger, Clarney's bullet scattered his brains. The very number of the attackers hindered their onslaught on the big Afridi, whose tigerish quickness made shooting as dangerous to themselves as to him. The bulk of them swarmed about him, striking with scimitar and rifle-stock while others charged up the steps after Steve. At that range there was no missing; the American simply thrust his rifle muzzle into a bearded face and blasted it into a ghastly ruin. The others came on, screaming like panthers.

And now as he prepared to expend his last cartridge, Clarney saw two things in one flashing instant—a wild warrior who, with froth on his beard and a heavy scimitar uplifted, was almost upon him, and another who knelt on the floor drawing a careful bead on the plunging Yar Ali. Steve made an instant choice and fired over the shoulder of the charging swordsman, killing the rifleman—and voluntarily offering his own life for his friend's; for the scimitar was swinging at his own head. But even as the Arab swung, grunting with the force of the blow, his sandaled foot slipped on the marble steps and the curved blade, veering erratically from its arc, clashed on Steve's rifle-barrel. In an instant the American clubbed his rifle, and as the Bedouin recovered his balance and again heaved up the scimitar, Clarney struck with all his rangy power, and stock and skull shattered together.

Then a heavy ball smacked into his shoulder, sickening him with the shock.

As he staggered dizzily, a Bedouin whipped a turban-cloth about his feet and jerked viciously. Clarney pitched headlong down the steps, to strike with stunning force. A gun-stock in a brown hand went up to dash out his brains, but an imperious command halted the blow.

"Slay him not, but bind him hand and foot."

As Steve struggled dazedly against many gripping

The Fire of Asshurbanipal

hands, it seemed to him that somewhere he had heard that imperious voice before.

The American's downfall had occurred in a matter of seconds. Even as Steve's second shot had cracked, Yar Ali had half severed a raider's arm and himself received a numbing blow from a rifle-stock on his left shoulder. His sheepskin coat, worn despite the desert heat, saved his hide from half a dozen slashing knives. A rifle was discharged so close to his face that the powder burnt him fiercely, bringing a bloodthirsty yell from the maddened Afghan. As Yar Ali swung up his dripping blade the rifleman, ashy-faced, lifted his rifle above his head in both hands to parry the downward blow, whereat the Afridi, with a yelp of ferocious exultation, shifted as a jungle-cat strikes and plunged his long knife into the Arab's belly. But at that instant a rifle-stock, swung with all the hearty ill-will its wielder could evoke, crashed against the giant's head, laying open the scalp and dashing him to his knees.

With the dogged and silent ferocity of his breed, Yar Ali staggered blindly up again, slashing at foes he could scarcely see, but a storm of blows battered him down again, nor did his attackers cease beating him until he lay still. They would have finished him in short order then but for another peremptory order from their chief; whereupon they bound the senseless knife-man and flung him down alongside Steve, who was fully conscious and aware of the savage hurt of the bullet in his shoulder.

He glared up at the tall Arab who stood looking down at him.

"Well, *sahib*," said this one—and Steve saw he was no Bedouin—"do you not remember me?"

Steve scowled; a bullet-wound is no aid to concentration.

"You look familiar—by Judas!—you are! Nureddin El Mekru!"

"I am honored! The *sahib* remembers!" Nureddin salaamed mockingly. "And you remember, no doubt, the occasion on which you made me a present of—this?"

The Fire of Asshurbanipal

The dark eyes shadowed with bitter menace and the shaykh indicated a thin white scar on the angle of his jaw.

"I remember," snarled Clarney, whom pain and anger did not tend to make docile. "It was in Somaliland, years ago. You were in the slave-trade then. A wretch of a nigger escaped from you and took refuge with me. You walked into my camp one night in your high-handed way, started a row and in the ensuing scrap you got a butcher-knife across your face. I wish I'd cut your lousy throat."

"You had your chance," answered the Arab. "Now the tables are turned."

"I thought your stamping-ground lay west," growled Clarney; "Yemen and the Somali country."

"I quit the slave-trade long ago," answered the shaykh. "It is an outworn game. I led a band of thieves in Yemen for a time; then again I was forced to change my location. I came here with a few faithful followers, and by Allah, those wild men nearly slit my throat at first. But I overcame their suspicions, and now I lead more men than have followed me in years.

"They whom you fought off yesterday were my men—scouts I had sent out ahead. My oasis lies far to the west. We have ridden for many days, for I was on my way to this very city. When my scouts rode in and told me of two wanderers, I did not alter my course, for I had business first in Beled-el-Djinn. We rode into the city from the west and saw your tracks in the sand. We followed them, and you were blind buffalo who heard not our coming."

Steve snarled. "You wouldn't have caught us so easy, only we thought no Bedouin would dare come into Kara-Shehr."

Nureddin nodded. "But I am no Bedouin. I have traveled far and seen many lands and many races, and I have read many books. I know that fear is smoke, that the dead are dead, and that djinn and ghosts and curses are mists that the wind blows away. It was because of the tales of the red stone that I came into this forsaken desert. But

The Fire of Asshurbanipal

it has taken months to persuade my men to ride with me here.

"But—I am here! And your presence is a delightful surprise. Doubtless you have guessed why I had you taken alive; I have more elaborate entertainment planned for you and that Pathan swine. Now—I take the Fire of Asshurbanipal and we will go."

He turned toward the dais, and one of his men, a bearded one-eyed giant, exclaimed, "Hold, my lord! Ancient evil reigned here before the days of Muhammad! The djinn howl through these halls when the winds blow, and men have seen ghosts dancing on the walls beneath the moon. No man of mortals has dared this black city for a thousand years—save one, half a century ago, who fled shrieking.

"You have come here from Yemen; you do not know the ancient curse on this foul city, and this evil stone, which pulses like the red heart of Satan! We have followed you here against our judgment, because you have proven yourself a strong man, and have said you hold a charm against all evil beings. You said you but wished to look on this mysterious gem, but now we see it is your intention to take it for yourself. Do not offend the djinn!"

"Nay, Nureddin, do not offend the djinn!" chorused the other Bedouins. The shaykh's own hard-bitten ruffians, standing in a compact group somewhat apart from the Bedouins, said nothing; hardened to crimes and deeds of impiety, they were less affected by the superstitions of the desert men, to whom the dread tale of the accursed city had been repeated for centuries. Steve, even while hating Nureddin with concentrated venom, realized the magnetic power of the man, the innate leadership that had enabled him to overcome thus far the fears and traditions of ages.

"The curse is laid on infidels who invade the city," answered Nureddin, "not on the Faithful. See, in this chamber have we overcome our *kafar* foes!"

A white-bearded desert hawk shook his head.

93

The Fire of Asshurbanipal

"The curse is more ancient than Muhammad, and recks not of race or creed. Evil men reared this black city in the dawn of the Beginnings of Days. They oppressed our ancestors of the black tents, and warred among themselves; aye, the black walls of this foul city were stained with blood, and echoed to the shouts of unholy revel and the whispers of dark intrigues.

"Thus came the stone to the city; there dwelt a magician at the court of Asshurbanipal, and the black wisdom of ages was not denied to him. To gain honor and power for himself, he dared the horrors of a nameless vast cavern in a dark, untraveled land, and from those fiend-haunted depths he brought that blazing gem, which is carved of the frozen flames of Hell! By reason of his fearful power in black magic, he put a spell on the demon which guarded the ancient gem, and so stole away the stone. And the demon slept in the cavern unknowing.

"So this magician—Xuthltan by name—dwelt in the court of the sultan Asshurbanipal and did magic and forecast events by scanning the lurid deeps of the stone, into which no eyes but his could look unblinded. And men called the stone the Fire of Asshurbanipal, in honor of the king.

"But evil came upon the kingdom and men cried out that it was the curse of the djinn, and the sultan in great fear bade Xuthltan take the gem and cast it into the cavern from which he had taken it, lest worse ill befall them.

"Yet it was not the magician's will to give up the gem wherein he read strange secrets of pre-Adamite days, and he fled to the rebel city of Kara-Shehr, where soon civil war broke out and men strove with one another to possess the gem. Then the king who ruled the city, coveting the stone, seized the magician and put him to death by torture, and in this very room he watched him die; with the gem in his hand the king sat upon the throne—even as he has sat upon the throne—even as he has sat throughout the centuries—even as now he sits!"

The Arab's finger stabbed at the moldering bones on the marble throne, and the wild desert men blenched;

The Fire of Asshurbanipal

even Nureddin's own scoundrels recoiled, catching their breath, but the shaykh showed no sign of perturbation.

"As Xuthltan died," continued the old Bedouin, "he cursed the stone whose magic had not saved him, and he shrieked aloud the fearful words which undid the spell he had put upon the demon in the cavern, and set the monster free. And crying out on the forgotten gods, Cthulhu and Koth and Yog-Sothoth, and all the pre-Adamite Dwellers in the black cities under the sea and the caverns of the earth, he called upon them to take back that which was theirs, and with his dying breath pronounced doom on the false king, and that doom was that the king should sit on his throne holding in his hand the Fire of Asshurbanipal until the thunder of Judgment Day.

"Thereat the great stone cried out as a live thing cries, and the king and his soldiers saw a black cloud spinning up from the floor, and out of the cloud blew a fetid wind, and out of the wind came a grisly shape which stretched forth fearsome paws and laid them on the king, who shriveled and died at their touch. And the soldiers fled screaming, and all the people of the city ran forth wailing into the desert, where they perished or gained through the wastes to the far oasis towns. Kara-Shehr lay silent and deserted, the haunt of the lizard and the jackal. And when some of the desert-people ventured into the city they found the king dead on his throne, clutching the blazing gem, but they dared not lay hand upon it, for they knew the demon lurked near to guard it through all the ages—as he lurks near even as we stand here."

The warriors shuddered involuntarily and glanced about, and Nureddin said, "Why did he not come forth when the Franks entered the chamber? Is he deaf, that the sound of the combat has not awakened him?"

"We have not touched the gem," answered the old Bedouin, "nor had the Franks molested it. Men have looked on it and lived; but no mortal may touch it and survive."

The Fire of Asshurbanipal

Nureddin started to speak, gazed at the stubborn, uneasy faces and realized the futility of argument. His attitude changed abruptly.

"I am master here," he snapped, dropping a hand to his holster. "I have not sweat and bled for this gem to be balked at the last by groundless fears! Stand back, all! Let any man cross me at the peril of his head!"

He faced them, his eyes blazing, and they fell back, cowed up the force of his ruthless personality. He strode boldly by the marble steps, and the Arabs caught their breath, recoiling toward the door; Yar Ali, conscious at last, groaned dismally. God! thought Steve, what a barbaric scene!—bound captives on the dust-heaped floor, wild warriors clustered about, gripping their weapons, the raw acrid scent of blood and burnt powder still fouling the air, corpses strewn in a horrid welter of blood, brains and entrails—and on the dais, the hawk-faced shaykh, oblivious to all except the evil crimson glow in the skeleton fingers that rested on the marble throne.

A tense silence gripped all as Nureddin stretched forth his hand slowly, as if hypnotized by the throbbing crimson light. And in Steve's subconsciousness there shuddered a dim echo, as of something vast and loathsome waking suddenly from an age-long slumber. The American's eyes moved instinctively toward the grim cyclopean walls. The jewel's glow had altered strangely; it burned a deeper, darker red, angry and menacing.

"Heart of all evil," murmured the shaykh, "how many princes died for thee in the Beginnings of Happenings? Surely the blood of kings throbs in thee. The sultans and the princesses and the generals who wore thee, they are dust and are forgotten, but thou blazest with majesty undimmed, fire of the world——"

Nureddin seized the stone. A shuddery wail broke from the Arabs, cut through by a sharp inhuman cry. To Steve it seemed, horribly, that the great jewel had cried out like a living thing! The stone slipped from the

The Fire of Asshurbanipal

shaykh's hand. Nureddin might have dropped it; to Steve it looked as though it leaped convulsively, as a live thing might leap. It rolled from the dais, bounding from step to step, with Nureddin springing after it, cursing as his clutching hand missed it. It struck the floor, veered sharply, and despite the deep dust, rolled like a revolving ball of fire toward the back wall. Nureddin was close upon it—it struck the wall—the shaykh's hand reached for it.

A scream of mortal fear ripped the tense silence. Without warning the solid wall had opened. Out of the black wall that gaped there, a tentacle shot and gripped the shaykh's body as a python girdles its victim, and jerked him headlong into the darkness. And then the wall showed blank and solid once more; only from within sounded a hideous, high-pitched, muffled screaming that chilled the blood of the listeners. Howling wordlessly, the Arabs stampeded, jammed in a battling, screeching mass in the doorway, tore through and raced madly down the wide stairs.

Steve and Yar Ali, lying helplessly, heard the frenzied clamor of their flight fade away into the distance, and gazed in dumb horror at the grim wall. The shrieks had faded into a more horrific silence. Holding their breath, they heard suddenly a sound that froze the blood in their veins—the soft sliding of metal or stone in a groove. At the same time the hidden door began to open, and Steve caught a glimmer in the blackness that might have been the glitter of monstrous eyes. He closed his own eyes; he dared not look upon whatever horror slunk from that hideous black well. He knew that there are strains the human brain cannot stand, and every primitive instinct in his soul cried out to him that this thing was nightmare and lunacy. He sensed that Yar Ali likewise closed his eyes, and the two lay like dead men.

Clarney heard no sound, but he sensed the presence of a horrific evil too grisly for human comprehension—of an Invader from Outer Gulfs and far black reaches of

The Fire of Asshurbanipal

cosmic being. A deadly cold pervaded the chamber, and Steve felt the glare of inhuman eyes sear through his closed lids and freeze his consciousness. If he looked, if he opened his eyes, he knew stark black madness would be his instant lot.

He felt a soul-shakingly foul breath against his face and knew that the monster was bending close above him, but he lay like a man frozen in a nightmare. He clung to one thought: neither he nor Yar Ali had touched the jewel this horror guarded.

Then he no longer smelled the foul odor, the coldness in the air grew appreciably less, and he heard again the secret door slide in its groove. The fiend was returning to its hiding-place. Not all the legions of Hell could have prevented Steve's eyes from opening a trifle. He had only a glimpse as the hidden door slid to—and that one glimpse was enough to drive all consciousness from his brain. Steve Clarney, iron-nerved adventurer, fainted for the only time in his checkered life.

How long he lay there Steve never knew, but it could not have been long, for he was roused by Yar Ali's whisper, "Lie still, *sahib*, a little shifting of my body and I can reach thy cords with my teeth."

Steve felt the Afghan's powerful teeth at work on his bonds, and as he lay with his face jammed into the thick dust, and his wounded shoulder began to throb agonizingly—he had forgotten it until now—he began to gather the wandering threads of his consciousness, and it all came back to him. How much, he wondered dazedly, had been the nightmares of delirium, born from suffering and the thirst that caked his throat? The fight with the Arabs had been real—the bonds and the wounds showed that—but the grisly doom of the shaykh—the thing that had crept out of the black entrance in the wall—surely that had been a figment of delirium. Nureddin had fallen into a well or pit of some sort—Steve felt his hands were free and he rose to a sitting posture, fumbling for a pocket-knife the Arabs had overlooked. He did not look up or about the chamber as he slashed the cords that

The Fire of Asshurbanipal

bound his ankles, and then freed Yar Ali, working awkwardly because his left arm was stiff and useless.

"Where are the Bedouins?" he asked, as the Afghan rose, lifting him to his feet.

"Allah, *sahib*," whispered Yar Ali, "are you mad? Have you forgotten? Let us go quickly before the djinn returns!"

"It was a nightmare," muttered Steve. "Look—the jewel is back on the throne——" His voice died out. Again that red glow throbbed about the ancient throne, reflecting from the moldering skull; again in the outstretched finger-bones pulsed the Fire of Asshurbanipal. But at the foot of the throne lay another object that had not been there before—the severed head of Nureddin el Mekru stared sightlessly up at the gray light filtering through the stone ceiling. The bloodless lips were drawn back from the teeth in a ghastly grin, the staring eyes mirrored an intolerable horror. In the thick dust of the floor three spoors showed—one of the shaykh's where he had followed the red jewel as it rolled to the wall, and above it two other sets of tracks, coming to the throne and returning to the wall—vast, shapeless tracks, as of splayed feet, taloned and gigantic, neither human nor animal.

"My God!" choked Steve. "It was true—and the Thing—the Thing I saw——"

Steve remembered the flight from that chamber as a rushing nightmare, in which he and his companion hurtled headlong down an endless stair that was a gray well of fear, raced blindly through dusty silent chambers, past the glowering idol in the mighty hall and into the blazing light of the desert sun, where they fell slavering, fighting for breath.

Again Steve was roused by the Afridi's voice: "*Sahib, sahib*, in the Name of Allah the Compassionate, our luck has turned!"

Steve looked at this companion as a man might look in a trance. The big Afghan's garments were in tatters, and blood-soaked. He was stained with dust and caked with

The Fire of Asshurbanipal

blood, and his voice was a croak. But his eyes were alight with hope and he pointed with a trembling finger.

"In the shade of yon ruined wall!" he croaked, striving to moisten his blackened lips. *"Allah il allah!* The horses of the men we killed! With canteens and food-pouches at the saddle-horns! Those dogs fled without halting for the steeds of their comrades!"

New life surged up into Steve's bosom and he rose, staggering.

"Out of here," he mumbled. "Out of here, quick!"

Like dying men they stumbled to the horses, tore them loose and climbed fumblingly into the saddles.

"We'll lead the spare mounts," croaked Steve, and Yar Ali nodded emphatic agreement.

"Belike we shall need them ere we sight the coast."

Though their tortured nerves screamed for the water that swung in canteens at the saddle-horns, they turned the mounts aside and, swaying in the saddle, rode like flying corpses down the long sandy street of Kara-Shehr, between the ruined palaces and the crumbling columns, crossed the fallen wall and swept out into the desert. Not once did either glance back toward that black pile of ancient horror, nor did either speak until the ruins faded into the hazy distance. Then and only then did they draw rein and ease their thirst.

"Allah il allah!" said Yar Ali piously. "Those dogs have beaten me until it is as though every bone in my body were broken. Dismount, I beg thee, *sahib*, and let me probe for that accursed bullet, and dress thy shoulder to the best of my meager ability."

While this was going on, Yar Ali spoke, avoiding his friend's eye. "You said, *sahib*, you said something about—about seeing? What saw ye, in Allah's name?"

A strong shudder shook the American's steely frame.

"You didn't look when—when the—the Thing put back the jewel in the skeleton's hand and left Nureddin's head on the dais?"

"By Allah, not I!" swore Yar Ali. "My eyes were as

closed as if they had been welded together by the molten irons of Satan!"

Steve made no reply until the comrades had once more swung into the saddle and started on their long trek for the coast, which, with spare horses, food, water and weapons, they had a good chance to reach.

"I looked," the American said somberly. "I wish I had not; I know I'll dream about it for the rest of my life. I had only a glance; I couldn't describe it as a man describes an earthly thing. God help me, it wasn't earthly or sane either. Mankind isn't the first owner of the earth; there were Beings here before his coming—and now, survivals of hideously ancient epochs. Maybe spheres of alien dimensions press unseen on this material universe today. Sorcerers have called up sleeping devils before now and controlled them with magic. It is not unreasonable to suppose an Assyrian magician could invoke an elemental demon out of the earth to avenge him and guard something that must have come out of Hell in the first place.

"I'll try to tell you what I glimpsed; then we'll never speak of it again. It was gigantic and black and shadowy; it was a hulking monstrosity that walked upright like a man, but it was like a toad, too, and it was winged and tentacled. I saw only its back; if I'd seen the front of it—its face—I'd have undoubtedly lost my mind. The old Arab was right; God help us, it was the monster that Xuthltan called up out of the dark blind caverns of the earth to guard the Fire of Asshurbanipal!"

The House of Arabu

To the house whence no one issues,
To the road from whence there is no return,
To the house whose inhabitants are deprived of light,
The place where dust is their nourishment, their food clay,
They have no light, dwelling in dense darkness,
And they are clothed, like birds, in a grament of feathers,
Where, over gate and bolt, dust is scattered.
—BABYLONIAN LEGEND OF ISHTAR

"Has he seen a night-spirit, is he listening to the whispers of them who dwell in darkness."

Strange words to be murmured in the feast-hall of Naram-ninub, amid the strain of lutes, the patter of fountains, and the tinkle of women's laughter. The great hall attested the wealth of its owner, not only by its vast dimensions, but by the richness of its adornment. The glazed surface of the walls offered a bewildering variegation of colors—blue, red, and orange enamels set off by squares of hammered gold. The air was heavy with incense, mingled with the fragrance of exotic blossoms from the gardens without. The feasters, silk-robed nobles of Nippur, lounged on satin cushions, drinking wine poured from alabaster vessels, and caressing the painted

The House of Arabu

and bejeweled playthings which Naram-ninub's wealth had brought from all parts of the East.

There were scores of these; their white limbs twinkled as they danced, or shone like ivory among the cushions where they sprawled. A jeweled tiara caught in a burnished mass of night-black hair, a gem-crusted armlet of massive gold, earrings of carven jade—these were their only garments. Their fragrance was dizzying. Shameless in their dancing, feasting and lovemaking, their light laughter filled the hall in waves of silvery sound.

On a broad cushion-piled dais reclined the giver of the feast, sensuously stroking the glossy locks of a lithe Arabian who had stretched herself on her supple belly beside him. His appearnace of sybaritic languor was belied by the vital sparkling of his dark eyes as he surveyed his guests. He was thick-bodied, with a short blue-black beard: a Semite—one of the many drifting yearly into Shumir.

With one exception his guests were Shumirians, shaven of chin and head. Their bodies were padded with rich living, their features smooth and placid. The exception among them stood out in startling contrast. Taller than they, he had none of their soft sleekness. He was made with the economy of relentless Nature. His physique was of the primitive, not of the civilized athlete. He was an incarnation of Power, raw, hard, wolfish—in the sinewy limbs, the corded neck, the great arch of the breast, the broad hard shoulders. Beneath his tousled golden mane his eyes were like blue ice. His strongly chiselled features reflected the wildness his frame suggested. There was about him nothing of the measured leisure of the other guests, but a ruthless directness in his every action. Whereas they sipped, he drank in great gulps. They nibbled at tid-bits, but he seized whole joints in his fingers and tore at the meat with his teeth. Yet his brow was shadowed, his expression moody. His magnetic eyes were introspective. Wherefore Prince Ibi-Engur lisped again in Naram-ninub's ear: "Has the lord Pyrrhas heard the whispering of night-things?"

The House of Arabu

Naram-ninub eyed his friend in some worriment. "Come, my lord," said he, "you are strangely distraught. Has any here done aught to offend you?"

Pyrrhas roused himself as from some gloomy meditation and shook his head. "Not so, friend; if I seem distracted it is because of a shadow that lies over my own mind." His accent was barbarous, but the timbre of his voice was strong and vibrant.

The others glanced at him in interest. He was Eannatum's general of mercenaries, an Argive whose saga was epic.

"Is it a woman, lord Pyrrhas?" asked Prince Enakalli with a laugh. Pyrrhas fixed him with his gloomy stare and the prince felt a cold wind blowing on his spine.

"Aye, a woman," muttered the Argive. "One who haunts my dreams and floats like a shadow between me and the moon. In my dreams I feel her teeth in my neck, and I wake to hear the flutter of wings and the cry of an owl."

A silence fell over the group on the dais. Only in the great hall below rose the babble of mirth and conversation and the tinkling of lutes, and a girl laughed loudly, with a curious note in her laughter.

"A curse is upon him," whispered the Arabian girl. Naram-ninub silenced her with a gesture, and was about to speak, when Ibi-Engur lisped: "My lord Pyrrhas, this has an uncanny touch, like the vengeance of a god. Have you done aught to offend a deity?"

Naram-ninub bit his lip in annoyance. It was well known that in his recent campaign against Erech, the Argive had cut down a priest of Anu in his shrine. Pyrrhas' maned head jerked up and he glared at Ibi-Engur as if undecided whether to attribute the remark to malice or lack of tact. The prince began to pale, but the slim Arabian rose to her knees and caught at Naram-ninub's arm.

"Look at Belibna!" She pointed at the girl who had laughed so wildly an instant before.

Her companions were drawing away from this girl

The House of Arabu

apprehensively. She did not speak to them, or seem to see them. She tossed her jeweled head and her shrill laughter rang through the feast-hall. Her slim body swayed back and forth, her bracelets clanged and jangled together as she tossed up her white arms. Her dark eyes gleamed with a wild light, her red lips curled with her unnatural mirth.

"The hand of Arabu is on her," whispered the Arabian uneasily.

"Belibna!" Naram-ninub called sharply. His only answer was another burst of wild laughter, and the girl cried stridently: "To the home of darkness, the dwelling of Irhalla; to the road whence there is no return; oh, Apsu, bitter is thy wine!" Her voice snapped in a terrible scream, and bounding from among her cushions, she leaped up on the dais, a dagger in her hand. Courtesans and guests shrieked and scrambled madly out of her way. But it was at Pyrrhas the girl rushed, her beautiful face a mask of fury. The Argive caught her wrist, and the abnormal strength of madness was futile against the barbarian's iron thews. He tossed her from him, and down the cushion-strewn steps, where she lay in a crumpled heap, her own dagger driven into her heart as she fell.

The hum of conversation which had ceased suddenly, rose again as the guards dragged away the body, and the painted dancers came back to their cushions. But Pyrrhas turned and taking his wide crimson cloak from a slave, threw it about his shoulders.

"Stay, my friend," urged Naram-ninub. "Let us not allow this small matter to interfere with our revels. Madness is common enough."

Pyrrhas shook his head irritably. "Nay, I'm weary of swilling and gorging. I'll go to my own house."

"Then the feasting is at an end," declared the Semite, rising and clapping his hands. "My own litter shall bear you to the house the king has given you—nay, I forgot you scorn the ride on other men's backs. Then I shall myself escort you home. My lords, will you accompany us?"

"Walk, like common men?" stuttered Prince Ur-

The House of Arabu

ilishu. "By Enlil, I will come. It will be a rare novelty. But I must have a slave to bear the train of my robe, lest it trail in the dust of the street. Come, friends, let us see the lord Pyrrhas home, by Ishtar!"

"A strange man," Ibi-Engur lisped to Libit-ishbi, as the party emerged from the spacious palace, and descended the broad tiled stair, guarded by bronze lions. "He walks the streets, unattended, like a very tradesman."

"Be careful," murmured the other. "He is quick to anger, and he stands high in the favor of Eannatum."

"Yet even the favored of the king had best beware of offending the god Anu," replied Ibi-Engur in an equally guarded voice.

The party were proceeding leisurely down the broad white street, gaped at by the common folk who bobbed their shaven heads as they passed. The sun was not long up, but the people of Nippur were well astir. There was much coming and going between the booths where the merchants spread their wares: a shifting panorama, woven of craftsmen, tradesmen, slaves, harlots, and soldiers in copper helmets. There went a merchant from his warehouse, a staid figure in sober woolen robe and white mantle; there hurried a slave in a linen tunic; there minced a painted hoyden whose short slit skirt displayed her sleek flank at every step. Above them the blue of the sky whitened with the heat of the mounting sun. The glazed surfaces of the buildings shimmered. They were flat-roofed, some of them three or four stories high. Nippur was a city of sun-dried brick, but its facings of enamel made it a riot of bright color.

Somewhere a priest was chanting: "Oh, Babbat, righteousness lifteth up to thee its head—"

Pyrrhas swore under his breath. They were passing the great temple of Enlil, towering up three hundred feet in the changeless blue sky.

"The towers stand against the sky like part of it," he swore, raking back a damp lock from his forehead. "The sky is enameled, and this is a world made by man."

The House of Arabu

"Nay, friend," demurred Naram-ninub. "Ea built the world from the body of Tiamat."

"I say men built Shumir!" exclaimed Pyrrhas, the wine he had drunk shadowing his eyes. "A flat land—a very banquet-board of a land—with rivers and cities painted upon it, and a sky of blue enamel over it. By Ymir, I was born in a land the gods built! There are great blue mountains, with valleys lying like long shadows between, and snow peaks glittering in the sun. Rivers rush foaming down the cliffs in everlasting tumult, and the broad leaves of the trees shake in the strong winds."

"I too, was born in a broad land, Pyrrhas," answered the Semite. "By night the desert lies white and awful beneath the moon, and by day it stretches in brown infinity beneath the sun. But it is in the swarming cities of men, these hives of bronze and gold and enamel and humanity, that wealth and glory lie."

Pyrrhas was about to speak, when a loud wailing attracted his attention. Down the street came a procession, bearing a carven and painted litter on which lay a figure hidden by flowers. Behind came a train of young women, their scanty garments rent, their black hair flowing wildly. They beat their naked bosoms and cried: "*Ailanu!* Thammuz is dead!" The throngs in the street took up the shout. The litter passed, swaying on the shoulders of the bearers; among the high-piled flowers shone the painted eyes of a carven image. The cry of the worshippers echoed down the street, dwindling in the distance.

Pyrrhas shrugged his mighty shoulders. "Soon they will be leaping and dancing and shouting, 'Adonis is living!', and the wenches who howl so bitterly now will give themselves to men in the streets for exultation. How many gods are there, in the devil's name?"

Naram-ninub pointed to the great zikkurat of Enlil, brooding over all like the brutish dream of a mad god.

"See ye the seven tiers: the lower black, the next of red enamel, the third blue, the fourth orange, the fifth yellow, while the sixth is faced with silver, and the seventh with pure gold which flames in the sunlight? Each stage in the temple symbolizes a deity: the sun, the moon, and the five planets Enlil and his tribe have set in the skies for their emblems. But Enlil is greater than all, and Nippur is his favored city."

"Greater than Anu?" muttered Pyrrhas, remembering a flaming shrine and a dying priest that gasped an awful threat.

"Which is the greatest leg of a tripod?" parried Naram-ninub.

Pyrrhas opened his mouth to reply, then recoiled with a curse, his sword flashing out. Under his very feet a serpent reared up, its forked tongue flickering like a jet of red lightning.

"What is it, friend?" Naram-ninub and the princes stared at him in surprise.

"What is it?" He swore. "Don't you see that snake—under your very feet? Stand aside and give me a clean swing at it—"

His voice broke off and his eyes clouded with doubt.

"It's gone," he muttered.

"I saw nothing," said Naram-ninub, and the others shook their heads, exchanging wondering glances.

The Argive passed his hand across his eyes, shaking his head.

"Perhaps it's the wine," he muttered. "Yet there was an adder, I swear by the heart of Ymir. I am accursed."

The others drew away from him, glancing at him strangely.

There had always been a restlessness in the soul of Pyrrhas the Argive, to haunt his dreams and drive him out on his long wanderings. It had brought him from the blue mountains of his race, southward into the fertile valleys and sea-fringing plains where rose the huts of the Mycenaeans; thence into the isle of Crete, where, in a rude town of rough stone and wood, a swart fishing people battered with the ships of Egypt; by those ships he had

The House of Arabu

gone into Egypt, where men toiled beneath the lash to rear the first pyramids, and where, in the ranks of the white-skinned mercenaries, the Shardana, he leanred the arts of war. But his wanderlust drove him again across the sea, to a mud-walled trading village on the coast of Asia, called Troy, whence he drifted southward into the pillage and carnage of Palestine where the original dwellers in the land were trampled under by the barbaric Canaanites out of the East. So by devious ways he came at last to the plains of Shumir, where city fought city, and the priests of a myriad rival gods intrigued and plotted, as they had done since the dawn of Time, and as they did for centuries after, until the rise of an obscure frontier town called Babylon exalted its city-god Merodach above all others as Bel-Marduk, the conqueror of Tiamat.

The bare outline of the saga of Pyrrhas the Argive is weak and paltry; it can not catch the echoes of the thundering pageantry that rioted through that saga: the feasts, revels, wars, the crash and splintering of ships and the onset of chariots. Let it suffice to say that the honor of kings was given to the Argive, and that in all Mesopotamia there was no man so feared as this golden-haired barbarian whose war-skill and fury broke the hosts of Erech on the field, and the yoke of Erech from the neck of Nippur.

From a mountain hut to a palace of jade and ivory Pyrrhas' saga had led him. Yet the dim half-animal dreams that had filled his slumber when he lay as a youth on a heap of wolfskins in his shaggy-headed father's hut were nothing so strange and monstrous as the dreams that haunted him on the silken couch in the palace of turquoise-towered Nippur.

It was from these dreams that Pyrrhas woke suddenly. No lamp burned in his chamber and the moon was not yet up, but the starlight filtered dimly through the casement. There was the vague outline of a lithe form, the gleam of an eye. Suddenly the night beat down oppressively hot and still. Pyrrhas heard the pound of his own blood through his veins. Why fear a woman lurking

The House of Arabu

in his chamber? But no woman's form was ever so pantherishly supple; no woman's eyes ever burned so in the darkness. With a gasping snarl he leaped from his couch and his sword hissed as it cut the air—but only the air. Something like a mocking laugh reached his ears, but the figure was gone.

A girl entered hastily with a lamp.

"Amytis! I saw *her!* It was no dream, this time! She laughed at me from the window!"

Amytis trembled as she set the lamp on an ebony table. She was a sleek sensuous creature, with long-lashed, heavy-lidded eyes, passionate lips, and a wealth of lustrous black curly locks. As she stood there naked the voluptuousness of her figure would have stirred the most jaded debauchee. A gift from Eannatum, she hated Pyrrhas, and he knew it, but found an angry gratification in possessing her. But now her hatred was drowned in her terror.

"It was Lilitu!" she stammered. "She has marked you for her own! She is the night-spirit, the mate of Ardat Lili. They dwell in the House of Arabu. You are accursed!"

His hands were bathed with sweat; molten ice seemed to be flowing sluggishly through his veins instead of blood.

"Where shall I turn? The priests hate and fear me since I burned Anu's temple."

"There is a man who is not bound by the priest-craft, and could aid you" she blurted out.

"Then tell me!" He was galvanized, trembling with eager impatience. "His name, girl! His name!"

But at this sign of weakness, her malice returned; she had blurted out what was in her mind, in her fear of the supernatural. Now all the vindictiveness in her was awake again.

"I have forgotten," she answered insolently, her eyes glowing with spite.

"Slut!" Gasping with the violence of his rage, he dragged her across a couch by her thick locks. Seizing his

The House of Arabu

sword-belt he wielded it with savage force, holding down the writhing naked body with his free hand. Each stroke was like the impact of a drover's whip. So mazed with fury was he, and she so incoherent with pain, that he did not at first realize that she was shrieking a name at the top of her voice. Recognizing this at last, he cast her from him, to fall in a whimpering heap on the mat-covered floor. Trembling and panting from the excess of his passion, he threw aside the belt and glared down at her.

"Gimil-ishbi, eh?"

"Yes!" she sobbed, grovelling on the floor in her excruciating anguish. "He was a priest of Enlil, until he turned diabolist and was banished. Ahhh, I faint! I swoon! Mercy! Mercy!"

"And where shall I find him?" he demanded.

"In the mound of Enzu, to the west of the city. Oh, Enlil, I am flayed alive! I perish!"

Turning from her, Pyrrhas hastily donned his garments and armor, without calling for a slave to aid him. He went forth, passed among his sleeping servitors without waking them, and secured the best of his horses. There were perhaps a score in all in Nippur, the property of the king and his wealthier nobles; they had been bought from the wild tribes far to the north, beyond the Caspian, whom in a later age men called Scythians. Each steed represented an actual fortune. Pyrrhas bridled the great beast and strapped on the saddle—merely a cloth pad, ornamented and richly worked.

The soldiers at the gate gaped at him as he drew rein and ordered them to open the great bronze portals, but they bowed and obeyed without question. His crimson cloak flowed behind him as he galloped through the gate.

"Enlil!" swore a soldier. "The Argive has drunk over-much of Naram-ninub's Egyptian wine."

"Nay," responded another; "did you see his face that it was pale, and his hand that it shook on the rein? The gods have touched him, and perchance he rides to the House of Arabu."

Shaking their helmeted heads dubiously, they

111

The House of Arabu

listened to the hoof-beats dwindling away in the west.

North, south and east from Nippur, farm-huts, villages and palm groves clustered the plain, threaded by the net-works of canals that connected the rivers. But westward the land lay bare and silent to the Euphrates, only charred expanses telling of former villages. A few moons ago raiders had swept out of the desert in a wave that engulfed the vineyards and huts and burst against the staggering walls of Nippur. Pyrrhas remembered the fighting along the walls, and the fighting on the plain, when his sally at the head of his phalanxes had broken the besiegers and driven them in headlong flight back across the Great River. Then the plain had been red with blood and black with smoke. Now it was already veiled in green again as the grain put forth its shoots, uncared for by man. But the toilers who had planted that grain had gone into the land of dusk and darkness.

Already the overflow from more populous districts was seeping back into the man-made waste. A few months, a year at most, and the land would again present the typical aspect of the Mesopotamian plain, swarming with villages, checked with tiny fields that were more like gardens than farms. Man would cover the scars man had made, and there would be forgetfulness, till the raiders swept again out of the desert. But now the plain lay bare and silent, the canals choked, broken and empty.

Here and there rose the remnants of palm groves, the crumbling ruins of villas and country palaces. Further out, barely visible under the stars, rose the mysterious hillock known as the mound of Enzu—the moon. It was not a natural hill, but whose hands had reared it and for what reason none knew. Before Nippur was built it had risen above the plain, and the nameless fingers that shaped it had vanished in the dust of time. To it Pyrrhas turned his horse's head.

And in the city he had left, Amytis furtively left his palace and took a devious course to a certain secret destination. She walked rather stiffly, limped, and

The House of Arabu

frequently paused to tenderly caress her person and lament over her injuries. But limping, cursing, and weeping, she eventually reached her destination, and stood before a man whose wealth and power was great in Nippur. His glance was an interrogation.

"He has gone to the Mound of the Moon, to speak with Gimil-ishbi," she said.

"Lilitu came to him again tonight," she shuddered, momentarily forgetting her pain and anger. "Truly he is accursed."

"By the priests of Anu?" His eyes narrowed to slits.

"So he suspects."

"And you?"

"What of me? I neither know nor care."

"Have you ever wondered why I pay you to spy upon him?" he demanded.

She shrugged her shoulders. "You pay me well; that is enough for me."

"Why does he go to Gimil-ishbi?"

"I told him the renegade might aid him against Lilitu."

Sudden anger made the man's face darkly sinister.

"I thought you hated him."

She shrank from the menace in the voice. "I spoke of the diabolist before I thought, and then he forced me to speak his name, curse him, I will not sit with ease for weeks!" Her resentment rendered her momentarily speechless.

The man ignored her, intent on his own somber meditations. At last he rose with sudden determination.

"I have waited too long," he muttered, like one speaking his thoughts aloud. "The fiends play with him while I bite my nails, and those who conspire with me grow restless and suspicious. Enlil alone knows what counsel Gimil-ishbi will give. When the moon rises I will ride forth and seek the Argive on the plain. A stab unaware—he will not suspect until my sword is through him. A bronze blade is surer than the powers of Darkness.

The House of Arabu

I was a fool to trust even a devil."

Amytis gasped with horror and caught at the velvet hangings for support.

"You? *You?*" Her lips framed a question too terrible to voice.

"Aye!" He accorded her a glance of grim amusement. With a gasp of terror she darted through the curtained door, her smarts forgotten in her fright.

Whether the cavern was hollowed by man or by Nature, none ever knew. At least its walls, floor and ceiling were symmetrical and composed of blocks of greenish stone, found nowhere else in that level land. Whatever its cause and origin, man occupied it now. A lamp hung from the rock roof, casting a weird light over the chamber and the bald pate of the man who sat crouching over a parchment scroll on a stone table before him. He looked up as a quick sure footfall sounded on the stone steps that led down into his abode. The next instant a tall figure stood framed in the doorway.

The man at the stone table scanned this figure with avid interest. Pyrrhas wore a hauberk of black leather and copper scales; his brazen greaves glinted in the lamplight. The wide crimson cloak, flung loosely about him, did not enmesh the long hilt that jutted from its folds. Shadowed by his horned bronze helmet, the Argive's eyes gleamed icily. So the warrior faced the sage.

Gimil-ishbi was very old. There was no leaven of Semitic blood in his withered veins. His bald head was round as a vulture's skull, and from it his great nose jutted like the beak of a vulture. His eyes were oblique, a rarity even in a pure-blooded Shumirian, and they were bright and black as beads. Whereas Pyrrhas' eyes were all depth, blue deeps and changing clouds and shadows, Gimil-ishbi's eyes were opaque as jet, and they never changed. His mouth was a gash whose smile was more terrible than its snarl.

He was clad in a simple black tunic, and his feet, in their cloth sandals, seemed strangely deformed. Pyrrhas

The House of Arabu

felt a curious twitching between his shoulder-blades as he glanced at those feet, and he drew his eyes away, and back to the sinister face.

"Deign to enter my humble abode, warrior," the voice was soft and silky, sounding strange from those harsh thin lips. "I would I could offer you food and drink, but I fear the food I eat and the wine I drink would find little favor in your sight." He laughed softly as at an obscure jest.

"I come not to eat or to drink," answered Pyrrhas abruptly, striding up to the table. "I come to buy a charm against devils."

"To buy?"

The Argive emptied a pouch of gold coins on the stone surface; they glistened dully in the lamplight. Gimil-ishbi's laugh was like the rustle of a serpent through dead grass.

"What is this yellow dirt to me? You speak of devils, and you bring me dust the wind blows away."

"Dust?" Pyrrhas scowled. Gimil-ishbi laid his hand on the shining heap and laughed; somewhere in the night an owl moaned. The priest lifted his hand. Beneath it lay a pile of yellow dust that gleamed dully in the lamplight. A sudden wind rushed down the steps, making the lamp flicker, whirling up the golden heap; for an instant the air was dazzled and spangled with the shining particles. Pyrrhas swore; his armor was sprinkled with yellow dust; it sparkled among the scales of his hauberk.

"Dust that the wind blows away," mumbled the priest. "Sit down, Pyrrhas of Nippur, and let us converse with each other."

Pyrrhas glanced about the narrow chamber; at the even stacks of clay tablets along the walls, and the rolls of papyrus above them. Then he seated himself on the stone bench opposite the priest, hitching his sword-belt so that its hilt was well to the front.

"You are far from the cradle of your race," said Gimil-ishbi. "You are the first golden-haired rover to tread the plains of Shumir."

115

The House of Arabu

"I have wandered in many lands," muttered the Argive, "but may the vultures pluck my bones if I ever saw a race so devil-ridden as this, or a land ruled and harried by so many gods and demons."

His gaze was fixed in fascination on Gimil-ishbi's hands; they were long, narrow, white and strong, the hands of youth. Their contrast to the priest's appearance of great age otherwise, was vaguely disquieting.

"To each city its gods and their priests," answered Gimil-ishbi; "and all fools. Of what account are gods whom the fortunes of men lift or lower? Behind all gods of men, behind the primal trinity of Ea, Anu and Enlil, lurk the elder gods, unchanged by the wars or ambitions of men. Men deny what they do not see. The priests of Eridu, which is sacred to Ea and light, are no blinder than them of Nippur, which is consecrated to Enlil, whom they deem the lord of Darkness. But he is only the god of the darkness of which men dream, not the real Darkness that lurks behind all dreams, and veils the real and awful deities. I glimpsed this truth when I was a priest of Enlil, wherefore they cast me forth. Ha! They would stare if they knew how many of their worshippers creep forth to me by night, as you have crept."

"I creep to no man!" The Argive bristled instantly. "I came to buy a charm. Name your price, and be damned to you."

"Be not wroth," smiled the priest. "Tell me why you have come."

"If you are so cursed wise you should know already," growled the Argive, unmollified. Then his gaze clouded as he cast back over his tangled trail. "Some magician has cursed me," he muttered. "As I rode back from my triumph over Erech, my war-horse screamed and shied at Something none saw but he. Then my dreams grew strange and monstrous. In the darkness of my chamber, wings rustled and feet padded stealthily. Yesterday a woman at a feast went mad and tried to knife me. Later an adder sprang out of empty air and struck at me. Then, this night, she men call Lilitu came to my

The House of Arabu

chamber and mocked me with awful laughter—"

"Lilitu?" the priest's eyes lit with a brooding fire; his skull-face worked in a ghastly smile. "Verily, warrior, thy plot they ruin in the House of Arabu. Your sword can not prevail against her, or against her mate Ardat Lili. In the gloom of midnight her teeth will find your throat. Her laugh will blast your ears, and her burning kisses will wither you like a dead leaf blowing in the hot winds of the desert. Madness and dissolution will be your lot, and you will descend to the House of Arabu whence none returns."

Pyrrhas moved restlessly, cursing incoherently beneath his breath.

"What can I offer you besides gold?" he growled.

"Much!" the black eyes shone; the mouth-gash twisted in inexplicable glee. "But I must name my own price, after I have given you aid."

Pyrrhas acquiesced with an impatient gesture.

"Who are the wisest men in the world?" asked the sage abruptly.

"The priests of Egypt, who scrawled on yonder parchments," answered the Argive.

Gimil-ishbi shook his head; his shadow fell on the wall like that of a great vulture, crouching over a dying victim.

"None so wise as the priests of Tiamat, who fools believe died long ago under the sword of Ea. Tiamat is deathless; she reigns in the shadows; she spreads her dark wings over her worshippers."

"I know them not," muttered Pyrrhas uneasily.

"The cities of men know them not; but the wasteplaces know them, the reedy marshes, the stony deserts, the hills, and the caverns. To them steal the winged ones from the House of Arabu."

"I thought none came from that House," said the Argive.

"No *human* returns thence. But the servants of Tiamat come and go at their pleasure."

Pyrrhas was silent, reflecting on the place of the dead, as believed in by the Shumirians; a vast cavern,

The House of Arabu

dusty, dark and silent, through which wandered the souls of the dead forever, shorn of all human attributes, cheerless and loveless, remembering their former lives only to hate all living men, their deeds and dreams.

"I will aid you," murmured the priest. Pyrrhas lifted his helmeted head and stared at him. Gimil-ishbi's eyes were no more human than the reflection of firelight on subterranean pools of inky blackness. His lips sucked in as if he gloated over all woes and miseries of mankind. Pyrrhas hated him as a man hates the unseen serpent in the darkness.

"Aid me and name your price," said the Argive.

Gimil-ishbi closed his hands and opened them, and in the palms lay a gold cask, the lid of which fastened with a jeweled catch. He sprung the lid, and Pyrrhas saw the cask was filled with grey dust. He shuddered without knowing why.

"This ground dust was once the skull of the first king of Ur," said Gimil-ishbi. "When he died, as even a necromancer must, he concealed his body with all his art. But I found his crumbling bones, and in the darkness above them, I fought with his soul as a man fights with a python in the night. My spoil was his skull, that held darker secrets than those that lie in the pits of Egypt.

"With this dead dust shall you trap Lilitu. Go quickly to an enclosed place—a cavern or a chamber—nay, that ruined villa which lies between this spot and the city will serve. Strew the dust in thin lines across threshold and window; leave not a spot as large as a man's hand unguarded. Then lie down as if in slumber. When Lilitu enters, as she will, speak the words I shall teach you. Then you are her master, until you free her again by repeating the conjure backwards. You can not slay her, but you can make her swear to leave you in peace. Make her swear by the dugs of Tiamat. Now lean close and I will whisper the words of the spell."

Somewhere in the night a nameless bird cried out harshly; the sound was more human than the whispering of the priest, which was no louder than the gliding of an

The House of Arabu

adder through slimy ooze. He drew back, his gash-mouth twisted in a grisly smile. The Argive sat for an instant like a statue of bronze. Their shadows fell together on the wall with the appearance of a crouching vulture facing a strange horned monster.

Pyrrhas took the cask and rose, wrapping his crimson cloak about his somber figure, his horned helmet lending an illusion of abnormal height.

"And the price?"

Gimil-ishbi's hands became claws, quivering with lust.

"Blood! A life!"

"Whose life?"

"Any life! So blood flows, and there is fear and agony, a spirit ruptured from its quivering flesh! I have one price for all—a human life! Death is my rapture; I would glut my soul on death! Man, maid or infant. You have sworn. Make good your oath! A life! A human life!"

"Aye, a life!" Pyrrhas' sword cut the air in a flaming arc and Gimil-ishbi's vulture head fell on the stone table. The body reared upright, spouting black blood, then slumped across the stone. The head rolled across the surface and thudded dully on the floor. The features stared up, frozen in a mask of awful surprise.

Outside there sounded a frightful scream as Pyrrhas' stallion broke its halter and raced madly away across the plain.

From the dim chamber with its tablets of cryptic cuneiforms and papyri of dark hieroglyphics, and from the remnants of the mysterious priest, Pyrrhas fled. As he climbed the carven stair and emerged into the starlight he doubted his own reason.

Far across the level plain the moon was rising, dull red, darkly lurid. Tense heat and silence held the land. Pyrrhas felt cold sweat thickly beading his flesh; his blood was a sluggish current of ice in his veins; his tongue clove to his palate. His armor weighted him and his cloak was like a clinging snare. Cursing incoherently he tore it from him; sweating and shaking he ripped off his armor, piece

The House of Arabu

by piece, and cast it away. In the grip of his abysmal fears he had reverted to the primitive. The veneer of civilization vanished. Naked but for loin-cloth and girded sword he strode across the plain, carrying the golden cask under his arm.

No sound disturbed the waiting silence as he came to the ruined villa whose walls reared drunkenly among heaps of rubble. One chamber stood above the general ruin, left practically untouched by some whim of chance. Only the door had been wrenched from its bronze hinges. Pyrrhas entered. Moonlight followed him in and made a dim radiance inside the portal. There were three windows, gold-barred. Sparingly he crossed the threshold with a thin grey line. Each casement he served in like manner. Then tossing aside the empty cask, he stretched himself on a bare dais that stood in deep shadow. His unreasoning horror was under control. He who had been the hunted was now the hunter. The trap was set, and he waited for his prey with the patience of the primitive.

He had not long to wait. Something threshed the air outside and the shadow of great wings crossed the moonlit portal. There was an instant of tense silence in which Pyrrhas heard the thunderous impact of his own heart against his ribs. Then a shadowy form framed itself in the open door. A fleeting instant it was visible, then it vanished from view. The thing had entered; the night-fiend was in the chamber.

Pyrrhas' hand clenched on his sword as he heaved up suddenly from the dais. His voice crashed in the stillness as he thundered the dark enigmatic conjurement whispered to him by the dead priest. He was answered by a frightful scream; there was a quick stamp of bare feet, then a heavy fall, and something was threshing and writhing in the shadows on the floor. As Pyrrhas cursed the masking darkness, the moon thrust a crimson rim above a casement, like a goblin peering into a window, and a molten flood of light crossed the floor. In the pale glow the Argive saw his victim.

But it was no were-woman that writhed there. It was

The House of Arabu

a thing like a man, lithe, naked, dusky-skinned. It differed not in the attributes of humanity except for the disquieting suppleness of its limbs, the changeless glitter of its eyes. It grovelled as in mortal agony, foaming at the mouth and contorting its body into impossible positions.

With a blood-mad yell Pyrrhas ran at the figure and plunged his sword through the squirming body. The point rang on the tiled floor beneath it, and an awful howl burst from the frothing lips, but that was the only apparent effect of the thrust. The Argive wrenched forth his sword and glared astoundedly to see no stain on the steel, no wound on the dusky body. He wheeled as the cry of the captive was re-echoed from without.

Just outside the enchanted threshold stood a woman, naked, supple, dusky, with wide eyes blazing in a soulless face. The being on the floor ceased to writhe, and Pyrrhas' blood turned to ice.

"Lilitu!"

She quivered at the threshold, as if held by an invisible boundary. Her eyes were eloquent with hate; they yearned awfully for his blood and his life. She spoke, and the effect of a human voice issuing from that beautiful unhuman mouth was more terrifying than if a wild beast had spoken in human tongue.

"You have trapped my mate! You dare to torture Ardat Lili, before whom the gods tremble! Oh, you shall howl for this! You shall be torn bone from bone, and muscle from muscle, and vein from vein! Loose him! Speak the words and set him free, lest even this doom be denied you!'

"Words!" he answered with bitter savagery. "You have hunted me like a hound. Now you can not cross that line without falling into my hands as your mate has fallen. Come into the chamber, bitch of darkness, and let me caress you as I caress your lover—thus—and thus!—and thus!"

Ardat Lili foamed and howled at the bite of the keen steel, and Lilitu screamed madly in protest, beating with her hands as at an invisible barrier.

The House of Arabu

"Cease! Cease! Oh, could I but come at you! How I would leave you a blind, mangled cripple! Have done! Ask what you will, and I will perform it!"

"That is well," grunted the Argive grimly. "I can not take this creature's life, but it seems I can hurt him, and unless you give me satisfaction, I will give him more pain than ever he guesses exists in the world."

"Ask! Ask!" urged the were-woman, twisting with impatience.

"Why have you haunted me? What have I done to earn your hate?"

"Hate?" she tossed her head. "What are the sons of men that we of Shuala should hate or love? When the doom is loosed, it strikes blindly."

"Then who, or what, loosed the doom of Lilitu upon me?"

"One who dwells in the House of Arabu."

"Why, in Ymir's name?" swore Pyrrhas. "Why should the dead hate me?" He halted, remembering a priest who died gurgling curses.

"The dead strike at the bidding of the living. Someone who moves in the sunlight spoke in the night to one who dwells in Shuala."

"Who?"

"I do not know."

"You lie, you slut! It is the priests of Anu, and you would shield them. For that lie your lover shall howl to the kiss of the steel—"

"Butcher!" shrieked Lilitu. "Hold your hand! I swear by the dugs of Tiamat my mistress, I do not know what you ask. What are the priests of Anu that I should shield them? I would rip up all their bellies—as I would yours, could I come at you! Free my mate, and I will lead you to the House of Darkness itself, and you may wrest the truth from the awful mouth of the dweller himself, if you dare!"

"I will go," said Pyrrhas, "but I leave Ardat Lili here as hostage. If you deal falsely with me, he will writhe on this enchanted floor throughout all eternity.

The House of Arabu

Lilitu wept with fury, crying: "No devil in Shuala is crueller than you. Haste, in the name of Apsu!"

Sheathing his sword, Pyrrhas stepped across the threshold. She caught his wrist with fingers like velvet-padded steel, crying something in a strange inhuman tongue. Instantly the moon-lit sky and plain were blotted out in a rush of icy blackness. There was a sensation of hurtling through a void of intolerable coldness, a roaring in the Argive's ears as of titan winds. Then his feet struck solid ground; stability followed that chaotic instant, that had been like the instant of dissolution that joins or separates two states of being, alike in stability, but in kind more alien than day and night. Pyrrhas knew that in that instant he had crossed an unimaginable gulf, and that he stood on shores never before touched by living human feet.

Lilitu's fingers grasped his wrist, but he could not see her. He stood in darkness of a quality which he had never encountered. It was almost tangibly soft, all-pervading and all-engulfing. Standing amidst it, it was not easy even to imagine sunlight and bright rivers and grass singing in the wind. They belonged to that other world—a world lost and forgotten in the dust of a million centuries. The world of life and light was a whim of chance—a bright spark glowing momentarily in a universe of dust and shadows. Darkness and silence were the natural state of the cosmos, not light and the noises of Life. No wonder the dead hated the living, who disturbed the grey stillness of Infinity with their tinkling laughter.

Lilitu's fingers drew him through abysmal blackness. He had a vague sensation as of being in a titanic cavern, too huge for conception. He sensed walls and roof, though he did not see them and never reached them; they seemed to recede as he advanced, yet there was always the sensation of their presence. Sometimes his feet stirred what he hoped was only dust. There was a dusty scent throughout the darkness; he smelled the odors of decay and mould.

He saw lights moving like glow-worms through the

The House of Arabu

dark. Yet they were not lights, as he knew radiance. They were most like spots of lesser gloom, that seemed to glow only by contrast with the engulfing blackness which they emphasized without illuminating. Slowly, laboriously they crawled through the eternal night. One approached the companions closely and Pyrrhas' hair stood up and he grasped his sword. But Lilitu took no heed as she hurried him on. The dim spot glowed close to him for an instant; it vaguely illumined a shadowy countenance, faintly human, yet strangely birdlike.

Existence became a dim and tangled thing to Pyrrhas, wherein he seemed to journey for a thousand years through the blackness of dust and decay, drawn and guided by the hand of the were-woman. Then he heard her breath hiss through her teeth, and she came to a halt.

Before them shimmered another of those strange globes of light. Pyrrhas could not tell whether it illumined a man or a bird. The creature stood upright like a man, but it was clad in grey feathers—at least they were more like feathers than anything else. The features were no more human than they were birdlike.

"This is the dweller in Shuala which put upon you the curse of the dead," whispered Lilitu. "Ask him the name of him who hates you on earth."

"Tell me the name of mine enemy!" demanded Pyrrhas, shuddering at the sound of his own voice, which whispered drearily and uncannily through the unechoing darkness.

The eyes of the dead burned redly and it came at him with a rustle of pinions, a long gleam of light springing into its lifted hand. Pyrrhas recoiled, clutching at his sword, but Lilitu hissed: "Nay, use this!" and he felt a hilt thrust into his fingers. He was grasping a scimitar with a blade curved in the shape of the crescent moon, that shone like an arc of white fire.

He parried the bird-thing's stroke, and sparks showered in the gloom, burning him like bits of flame. The darkness clung to him like a black cloak; the glow of the feathered monster bewildered and baffled him. It was

The House of Arabu

like fighting a shadow in the maze of a nightmare. Only by the fiery gleam of his enemy's blade did he keep the touch of it. Thrice it sang death in his ears as he deflected it by the merest fraction, then his own crescent-edge cut the darkness and grated on the other's shoulder-joint. With a strident screech the thing dropped its weapon and slumped down, a milky liquid spurting from the gaping wound. Pyrrhas lifted his scimitar again, when the creature gasped in a voice that was no more human than the grating of wind-blown boughs against one another: "Naram-ninub, the great-grandson of my great-grandson! By black arts he spoke and commanded me across the gulfs!"

"Naram-ninub!" Pyrrhas stood frozen in amazement; the scimitar was torn from his hand. Again Lilitu's fingers locked on his wrist. Again the dark was drowned in deep blackness and howling winds blowing between the spheres.

He staggered in the moonlight without the ruined villa, reeling with the dizziness of his transmutation. Beside him Lilitu's teeth shone between her curling red lips. Catching the thick locks clustered on her neck, he shook her savagely, as he would have shaken a mortal woman.

"Harlot of Hell! What madness has your sorcery instilled in my brain?"

"No madness!" she laughed, striking his hand aside. "You have journeyed to the House of Arabu, and you have returned. You have spoken with and overcome with the sword of Apsu, the shade of a man dead for long centuries."

"Then it was no dream of madness! But Naram-ninub—" he halted in confused thought. "Why, of all the men of Nippur, he has been my staunchest friend!"

"Friend?" she mocked. "What is friendship but a pleasant pretense to while away an idle hour?"

"But why, in Ymir's name?"

"What are the petty intrigues of men to me?" she exclaimed angrily. "Yet now I remember that men from

The House of Arabu

Erech, wrapped in cloaks, steal by night to Naram-ninub's palace."

"Ymir!" like a sudden blaze of light Pyrrhas saw reason in merciless clarity. "He would sell Nippur to Erech, and first he must put me out of the way, because the hosts of Nippur cannot stand before me! Oh, dog, let my knife find your heart!"

"Keep faith with me!" Lilitu's importunities drowned his fury. "I have kept faith with you. I have led you where never living man has trod, and brought you forth unharmed. I have betrayed the dwellers in darkness and done that for which Tiamat will bind me naked on a white-hot grid for seven times seven days. Speak the words and free Ardat Lili!"

Still engrossed in Naram-ninub's treachery, Pyrrhas spoke the incantation. With a loud sigh of relief, the were-man rose from the tiled floor and came into the moonlight. The Argive stood with his hand on his sword and his head bent, lost in moody thought. Lilitu's eyes flashed a quick meaning to her mate. Lithely they began to steal toward the abstracted man. Some primitive instinct brought his head up with a jerk. They were closing in on him, their eyes burning in the moonlight, their fingers reaching for him. Instantly he realized his mistake; he had forgotten to make them swear truce with him; no oath bound them from his flesh.

With feline screeches they struck in, but quicker yet he bounded aside and raced toward the distant city. Too hotly eager for his blood to resort to sorcery, they gave chase. Fear winged his feet, but close behind him he heard the swift patter of their feet, their eager panting. A sudden drum of hoofs sounded in front of him, and bursting through a tattered grove of skeleton palms, he almost caromed against a rider, who rode like the wind, a long silvery glitter in his hand. With a startled oath the horseman wrenched his steed back on its haunches. Pyrrhas saw looming over him a powerful body in scale-mail, a pair of blazing eyes that glared at him from under a domed helmet, a short black beard.

The House of Arabu

"You dog!" he yelled furiously. "Damn you, have you come to complete with your sword what your black magic began?"

The steed reared wildly as he leaped at its head and caught its bridle. Cursing madly and fighting for balance, Naram-ninub slashed at his attacker's head, but Pyrrhas parried the stroke and thrust upward murderously. The sword-point glanced from the corselet and plowed along the Semite's jaw-bone. Naram-ninub screamed and fell from the plunging steed, spouting blood. His leg-bone snapped as he pitched heavily to earth, and his cry was echoed by a gloating howl from the shadowed grove.

Without dragging the rearing horse to earth, Pyrrhas sprang to its back and wrenched it about. Naram-ninub was groaning and writhing on the ground, and as Pyrrhas looked, two shadows darted from the darkened grove and fastened themselves on his prostrate form. A terrible scream burst from his lips, echoed by more awful laughter. Blood on the night air; on it the night-things would feed, wild as mad dogs, making no difference between men.

The Argive wheeled away, toward the city, then hesitated, shaken by a fierce revulsion. The level land lay quiescent beneath the moon, and the brutish pyramid of Enlil stood up in the stars. Behind him lay his enemy, glutting the fangs of the horrors he himself had called up from the Pits. The road was open to Nippur, for his return.

His return?—to a devil-ridden people crawling beneath the heels of priest and king; to a city rotten with intrigue and obscene mysteries; to an alien race that mistrusted him, and a mistress that hated him.

Wheeling his horse again, he rode westward toward the open lands, flinging his arms wide in a gesture of renunciation and the exultation of freedom. The weariness of life dropped from him like a cloak. His mane floated in the wind, and over the plains of Shumir shouted a sound they had never heard before—the gusty, elemental, reasonless laughter of a free barbarian.

The Horror From The Mound

Steve Brill did not believe in ghosts or demons. Juan Lopez did. But neither the caution of the one nor the sturdy skepticism of the other was shield against the horror that fell upon them—the horror forgotten by men for more than three hundred years—a screaming fear monstrously resurrected from the black lost ages.

Yet as Steve Brill sat on his sagging stoop that last evening, his thoughts were as far from uncanny menaces as the thoughts of man can be. His ruminations were bitter but materialistic. He surveyed his farmland and he swore. Brill was tall, rangy and tough as boot-leather—true son of the iron-bodied pioneers who wrenched West Texas from the wilderness. He was browned by the sun and strong as a longhorned steer. His lean legs and the boots on them showed his cowboy instincts, and now he cursed himself that he had ever climbed off the hurricane deck of his crank-eyed mustang and turned to farming. He was no farmer, the young puncher admitted profanely.

Yet his failure had not all been his fault. Plentiful rain in the winter—so rare in West Texas—had given promise of good crops. But as usual, things had happened. A late blizzard had destroyed all the budding fruit. The grain which had looked so promising was

The Horror From The Mound

ripped to shreds and battered into the ground by terrific hailstorms just as it was turning yellow. A period of intense dryness, followed by another hailstorm, finished the corn.

Then the cotton, which had somehow struggled through, fell before a swarm of grasshoppers which stripped Brill's field almost overnight. So Brill sat and swore that he would not renew his lease—he gave fervent thanks that he did not own the land on which he had wasted his sweat, and that there were still broad rolling ranges to the West where a strong young man could make his living riding and roping.

Now as Brill sat glumly, he was aware of the approaching form of his nearest neighbor, Juan Lopez, a taciturn old Mexican who lived in a hut just out of sight over the hill across the creek, and grubbed for a living. At present he was clearing a strip of land on an adjoining farm, and in returning to his hut he crossed a corner of Brill's pasture.

Brill idly watched him climb through the barbed-wire fence and trudge along the path he had worn in the short dry grass. He had been working at his present job for over a month now, chopping down tough gnarly mesquite trees and digging up their incredibly long roots, and Brill knew that he always followed the same path home. And watching, Brill noted him swerving far aside, seemingly to avoid a low rounded hillock which jutted above the level of the pasture. Lopez went far around this knoll and Brill remembered that the old Mexican always circled it at a distance. And another thing came into Brill's idle mind—Lopez always increased his gait when he was passing the knoll, and he always managed to get by it before sundown—yet Mexican laborers generally worked from the first light of dawn to the last glint of twilight, especially at these grubbing jobs, when they were paid by the acre and not by the day. Brill's curiosity was aroused.

He rose, and sauntering down the slight slope on the crown of which his shack sat, hailed the plodding Mexican.

The Horror From The Mound

"Hey, Lopez, wait a minute."

Lopez halted, looked about, and remained motionless but unenthusiastic as the white man approached.

"Lopez," said Brill lazily, "it ain't none of my business, but I just wanted to ask you—how come you always go so far around that old Indian mound?"

"No sabe," grunted Lopez shortly.

"You're a liar," responded Brill genially. "You savvy all right; you speak English as good as me. What's the matter—you think that mound's ha'nted or somethin'!"

Brill could speak Spanish himself and read it, too, but like most Anglo-Saxons he much preferred to speak his own language.

Lopez shrugged his shoulders.

"It is not a good place, *no bueno,*" he muttered, avoiding Brill's eyes. "Let hidden things rest."

"I reckon you're scared of ghosts," Brill bantered. "Shucks, if that is an Indian mound, them Indians been dead so long their ghosts 'ud be plumb wore out by now."

Brill knew that the illiterate Mexicans looked with superstitious aversion on the mounds that are found here and there through the Southwest—relics of a past and forgotten age, containing the moldering bones of chiefs and warriors of a lost race.

"Best not to disturb what is hidden in the earth," grunted Lopez.

"Bosh," said Brill. "Me and some boys busted into one of them mounds over in the Palo Pinto country and dug up pieces of skeleton with some beads and flint arrowheads and the like. I kept some of the teeth a long time till I lost 'em, and I ain't never been ha'nted."

"Indians?" snorted Lopez unexpectedly. "Who spoke of Indians? There have been more than Indians in this country. In the old times strange things happened here. I have heard the tales of my people, handed down from generation to generation. And my people were here long before yours, Senor Brill."

"Yeah, you're right," admitted Steve. "First white

130

The Horror From The Mound

men in this country was Spaniards, of course. Coronado passed along not very far from here, I hear-tell, and Hernando de Estrada's expedition came through here—away back yonder—I dunno how long ago."

"In 1545," said Lopez. "They pitched camp yonder where your corral stands now."

Brill turned to glance at his rail-fenced corral, inhabited now by his saddlehorse, a pair of workhorses and a scrawny cow.

"How come you know so much about it?" he asked curiously.

"One of my ancestors marched with de Estrada," answered Lopez. "A soldier, Porfirio Lopez; he told his son of that expedition, and he told *his* son, and so down the family line to me, who have no son to whom I can tell the tale."

"I didn't know you were so well connected," said Brill. "Maybe you know somethin' about the gold de Estrada was supposed to have hid around here somewhere."

"There was no gold," growled Lopez. "De Estrada's soldiers bore only their arms, and they fought their way through hostile country—many left their bones along the trail. Later—many years later—a mule train from Sante Fe was attacked not many miles from here by Comanches and they hid their gold and escaped; so the legends got mixed up. But even their gold is not there now, because Gringo buffalo-hunters found it and dug it up."

Brill nodded abstractedly, hardly heeding. Of all the continent of North America there is no section so haunted by tales of lost or hidden treasure as is the Southwest. Uncounted wealth passed back and forth over the hills and plains of Texas and New Mexico in the old days when Spain owned the gold and silver mines of the New World and controlled the rich fur trade of the West, and echoes of that wealth linger on in tales of golden caches. Some such vagrant dream, born of failure and pressing poverty, rose in Brill's mind.

131

The Horror From The Mound

Aloud he spoke: "Well, anyway, I got nothin' else to do and I believe I'll dig into that old mound and see what I can find."

The effect of that simple statement on Lopez was nothing short of shocking. He recoiled and his swarthy brown face went ashy; his black eyes flared and he threw up his arms in a gesture of intense expostulation.

"Dios, no!" he cried. "Don't do that, Senor Brill! There is a curse—my grandfather told me—"

"Told you what?" asked Brill.

Lopez lapsed into sullen silence.

"I cannot speak," he muttered. "I am sworn to silence. Only to an eldest son could I open my heart. But believe me when I say better had you cut your throat than to break into that accursed mound."

"Well," said Brill, impatient of Mexican superstitions, "if it's so bad why don't you tell me about it? Gimme a logical reason for not bustin' into it."

"I cannot speak!" cried the Mexican desperately. "I *know!*—but I swore to silence on the Holy Crucifix, just as every man of my family has sworn. It is a thing so dark, it is to risk damnation even to speak of it! Were I to tell you, I would blast the soul from your body. But I have sworn—and I have no son, so my lips are sealed forever."

"Aw, well," said Brill sarcastically, "why don't you write it out?"

Lopez started, stared, and to Steve's surprise, caught at the suggestion.

"I will! *Dios* be thanked the good priest taught me to write when I was a child. My oath said nothing of writing. I only swore not to speak. I will write out the whole thing for you, if you will swear not to speak of it afterward, and to destroy the paper as soon as you have read it."

"Sure," said Brill, to humor him, and the old Mexican seemed much relieved.

"Bueno! I will go at once and write. Tomorrow as I go to work I will bring you the paper and you will understand why no one must open that accursed mound!"

And Lopez hurried along his homeward path, his

132

The Horror From The Mound

stooped shoulders swaying with the effort of his unwonted haste. Steve grinned after him, shrugged his shoulders and turned back toward his own shack. Then he halted, gazing back at the low rounded mound with its grass-grown sides. It must be an Indian tomb, he decided, what with its symmetry and its similarity to other Indian mounds he had seen. He scowled as he tried to figure out the seeming connection between the mysterious knoll and the martial ancestor of Juan Lopez.

Brill gazed after the receding figure of the old Mexican. A shallow valley, cut by a half-dry creek, bordered with trees and underbrush, lay between Brill's pasture and the low sloping hill beyond which lay Lopez's shack. Among the trees along the creek bank the old Mexican was disappearing. And Brill came to a sudden decision.

Hurrying up the slight slope, he took a pick and a shovel from the tool shed built onto the back of his shack. The sun had not yet set and Brill believed he could open the mound deep enough to determine its nature before dark. If not, he could work by lantern light. Steve, like most of his breed, lived mostly by impulse, and his present urge was to tear into that mysterious hillock and find what, if anything, was concealed therein. The thought of treasure came again to his mind, piqued by the evasive attitude of Lopez.

What if, after all, that grassy heap of brown earth hid riches—virgin ore from forgotten mines, or the minted coinage of old Spain? Was it not possible that the musketeers of de Estrada had themselves reared that pile above a treasure they could not bear away, molding it in the likeness of an Indian mound to fool seekers? Did old Lopez know that? It would not be strange if, knowing of treasure there, the old Mexican refrained from disturbing it. Ridden with grisly superstitious fears, he might well live out a life of barren toil rather than risk the wrath of lurking ghosts or devils—for the Mexicans say that hidden gold is always accursed, and surely there was supposed to be some especial doom resting on this

The Horror From The Mound

mound. Well, Brill meditated, Latin-Indian devils had no terrors for the Anglo-Saxon, tormented by the demons of drouth and storm and crop failure.

Steve set to work with the savage energy characteristic of his breed. The task was no light one; the soil, baked by the fierce sun, was iron-hard, and mixed with rocks and pebbles. Brill sweated profusely and grunted with his efforts, but the fire of the treasure-hunter was on him. He shook the sweat out of his eyes and drove in the pick with mighty strokes that ripped and crumbled the close-packed dirt.

The sun went down, and in the long dreamy summer twilight he worked on, almost oblivious of time or space. He began to be convinced that the mound was a genuine Indian tomb, as he found traces of charcoal in the soil. The ancient people which reared these sepulchers had kept fires burning upon them for days, at some point in the building. All the mounds Steve had ever opened had contained a solid stratum of charcoal a short distance below the surface. But the charcoal traces he found now were scattered about through the soil.

His idea of a Spanish-built treasure trove faded, but he persisted. Who knows? Perhaps that strange folk men now called Mound-Builders had treasure of their own which they laid away with the dead.

Then Steve yelped in exultation as his pick rang on a bit of metal. He snatched it up and held it close to his eyes, straining in the waning light. It was caked and corroded with rust, worn almost paper-thin, but he knew it for what it was—a spur-rowel, unmistakably Spanish with its long cruel points. And he halted, completely bewildered. No Spaniard ever reared this mound, with its undeniable marks of aboriginal workmanship. Yet how came that relic of Spanish caballeros hidden deep in the packed soil?

Brill shook his head and set to work again. He knew that in the center of the mound, if it were indeed an aboriginal tomb, he would find a narrow chamber built of heavy stones, containing the bones of the chief for whom the mound had been reared and the victims sacrificed

The Horror From The Mound

above it. And in the gathering darkness he felt his pick strike heavily against something granite-like and unyielding. Examination, by sense of feel as well as by sight, proved it to be a solid block of stone, roughly hewn. Doubtless it formed one of the ends of the death-chamber. Useless to try to shatter it. Brill chipped and pecked about it, scraping the dirt and pebbles away from the corners until he felt that wrenching it out would be but a matter of sinking the pick-point underneath and levering it out.

But now he was suddenly aware that darkness had come on. In the young moon objects were dim and shadowy. His mustang nickered in the corral whence came the comfortable crunch of tired beasts' jaws on corn. A whippoorwill called eerily from the dark shadows of the narrow winding creek. Brill straightened reluctantly. Better get a lantern and continue his explorations by its light.

He felt in his pocket with some idea of wrenching out the stone and exploring the cavity by the aid of matches. Then he stiffened. Was it imagination that he heard a faint sinister rustling, which seemed to come from behind the blocking stone? Snakes! Doubtless they had holes somewhere about the base of the mound and there might be a dozen big diamond-backed rattlers coiled up in that cave-like interior waiting for him to put his hand among them. He shivered slightly at the thought and backed away out of the excavation he had made.

It wouldn't do to go poking about blindly into holes. And for the past few minutes, he realized, he had been aware of a faint foul odor exuding from interstices about the blocking stone—though he admitted that the smell suggested reptiles no more than it did any other menacing scent. It had a charnel-house reek about it—gases formed in the chamber of death, no doubt, and dangerous to the living.

Steve laid down his pick and returned to the house, impatient of the necessary delay. Entering the dark building, he struck a match and located his kerosene

The Horror From The Mound

lantern hanging on its nail on the wall. Shaking it, he satisfied himself that it was nearly full of coal oil, and lighted it. Then he fared forth again, for his eagerness would not allow him to pause long enough for a bite of food. The mere opening of the mound intrigued him, as it must always intrigue a man of imagination, and the discovery of the Spanish spur had whetted his curiosity.

He hurried from his shack, the swinging lantern casting long distorted shadows ahead of him and behind. He chuckled as he visualized Lopez's thoughts and actions when he learned, on the morrow, that the forbidden mound had been pried into. A good thing he opened it that evening, Brill reflected; Lopez might even have tried to prevent him meddling with it, had he known.

In the dreamy hush of the summer night, Brill reached the mound—lifted his lantern—swore bewilderedly. The lantern revealed his excavations, his tools lying carelessly where he had dropped them—and a black gaping aperture! The great blocking stone lay in the bottom of the excavation he had made, as if thrust carelessly aside. Warily he thrust the lantern forward and peered into the small cave-like chamber, expecting to see he knew not what. Nothing met his eyes except the bare rock sides of a long narrow cell, large enough to receive a man's body, which had apparently been built up of roughly hewn square-cut stones, cunningly and strongly joined together.

"Lopez!" exclaimed Steve furiously "The dirty coyote! He's been watchin' me work—and when I went after the lantern, he snuck up and pried the rock out—and grabbed whatever was in there, I reckon. Blast his greasy hide, I'll fix him!"

Savagely he extinguished the lantern and glared across the shallow, brush-grown valley. And as he looked he stiffened. Over the corner of the hill, on the other side of which the shack of Lopez stood, a shadow moved. The slender moon was setting, the light dim and the play of the shadows baffling. But Steve's eyes were sharpened by the sun and winds of the wastelands, and he knew that it was

The Horror From The Mound

some two-legged creature that was disappearing over the low shoulder of the mesquite-grown hill.

"Beatin' it to his shack," snarled Brill. "He's shore got somethin' or he wouldn't be travelin' at that speed."

Brill swallowed, wondering why a peculiar trembling had suddenly taken hold of him. What was there unusual about a thieving old greaser running home with his loot? Brill tried to drown the feeling that there was something peculiar about the gait of the dim shadow, which had seemed to move at a sort of slinking lope. There must have been need for swiftness when stocky old Juan Lopez elected to travel at such a strange pace.

"Whatever he found is as much mine as his," swore Brill, trying to get his mind off the abnormal aspect of the figure's flight, "I got this land leased and I done all the work diggin'. A curse, heck! No wonder he told me that stuff. Wanted me to leave it alone so he could get it hisself. It's a wonder he ain't dug it up long before this. But you can't never tell about them spigs."

Brill, as he meditated thus, was striding down the gentle slope of the pasture which led down to the creek bed. He passed into the shadows of the trees and dense underbrush and walked across the dry creek bed, noting absently that neither whippoorwill nor hoot-owl called in the darkness. There was a waiting, listening tenseness in the night that he did not like. The shadows in the creek bed seemed too thick, too breathless. He wished he had not blown out the lantern, which he still carried, and was glad he had brought the pick, gripped like a battle-ax in his right hand. He had an impulse to whistle, just to break the silence, then swore and dismissed the thought. Yet he was glad when he clambered up the low opposite bank and emerged into the starlight.

He walked up the slope and onto the hill, and looked down on the mesquite flat wherein stood Lopez's squalid hut. A light showed at the one window.

"Packin' his things for a getaway, I reckon," grunted Steve. "Oh, what the—"

He staggered as from a physical impact as a frightful

137

The Horror From The Mound

scream knifed the stillness. He wanted to clap his hands over his ears to shut out the horror of that cry, which rose unbearably and then broke in an abhorrent gurgle.

"Good God!" Steve felt the cold sweat spring out upon him. "Lopez—or somebody—"

Even as he gasped the words he was running down the hill as fast as his long legs could carry him. Some unspeakable horror was taking place in that lonely hut, but he was going to investigate it if it meant facing the Devil himself. He tightened his grip on his pick-handle as he ran. Wandering prowlers, murdering old Lopez for the loot he had taken from the mound, Steve thought, and forgot his wrath. It would go hard for anyone he found molesting the old scoundrel, thief though he might be.

He hit the flat, running hard. And then the light in the hut went out and Steve staggered in full flight, bringing up against a mesquite tree with an impact that jolted a grunt out of him and tore his hands on the thorns. Rebounding with a sobbed curse, he rushed for the shack, nerving himself for what he might see—his hair still standing on end at what he had already seen.

Brill tried the one door of the hut and found it bolted. He shouted to Lopez and received no answer. Yet utter silence did not reign. From within came a curious muffled worrying sound that ceased as Brill swung his pick crashing against the door. The flimsy portal splintered and Brill leaped into the dark hut, eyes blazing, pick swung high for a desperate onslaught. But no sound ruffled the grisly silence, and in the darkness nothing stirred, though Brill's chaotic imagination peopled the shadowed corners of the hut with the shapes of horror.

With a hand damp with perspiration he found a match and struck it. Besides himself only Lopez occupied the hut—old Lopez, stark dead on the dirt floor, arms spread wide like a crucifix, mouth sagging open in a semblance of idiocy, eyes wide and staring with a horror Brill found intolerable. The one window gaped open, showing the method of the slayer's exit—possibly his

The Horror From The Mound

entrance as well. Brill went to that window and gazed out warily. He saw only the sloping hillside on one hand and the mesquite flat on the other. He started—was that a hint of movement among the stunted shadows of the mesquites and chaparral—or had he but imagined he glimpsed a dim loping figure among the trees?

He turned back, as the match burned down to his fingers. He lit the old coal-oil lamp on the rude table, cursing as he burned his hand. The globe of the lamp was very hot, as if it had been burning for hours.

Reluctantly he turned to the corpse on the floor. Whatever sort of death had come to Lopez, it had been horrible, but Brill, gingerly examining the dead man, found no wound—no mark of knife or bludgeon on him. Wait! There was a thin smear of blood on Brill's questing hand. Searching, he found the source—three or four tiny punctures in Lopez's throat, from which blood had oozed sluggishly. At first he thought they had been inflicted with a stiletto—a thin round edgeless dagger—then he shook his head. He had seen stiletto wounds—he had the scar of one on his own body. These wounds more resembled the bite of some animal—they looked like the marks of pointed fangs.

Yet Brill did not believe they were deep enough to have caused death, nor had much blood flowed from them. A belief, abhorrent with grisly speculations, rose up in the dark corners of his mind—that Lopez had died of fright, and that the wounds had been inflicted either simultaneously with his death, or an instant afterward.

And Steve noticed something else; scrawled about on the floor lay a number of dingy leaves of paper, scrawled in the old Mexican's crude hand—he would write of the curse on the mound, he had said. There were the sheets on which he had written, there was the stump of a pencil on the floor, there was the hot lamp globe, all mute witnesses that the old Mexican had been seated at the rough-hewn table writing for hours. Then it was not he who opened the mound-chamber and stole the

The Horror From The Mound

contents—but who was it, in God's name? And who or what was it that Brill had glimpsed loping over the shoulder of the hill?

Well, there was but one thing to do—saddle his mustang and ride the ten miles to Coyote Wells, the nearest town, and inform the sheriff of the murder.

Brill gathered up the papers. The last was crumpled in the old man's clutching hand and Brill secured it with some difficulty. Then as he turned to extinguish the light, he hesitated, and cursed himself for the crawling fear that lurked at the back of his mind—fear of the shadowy thing he had seen cross the window just before the light was extinguished in the hut. The long arm of the murderer, he thought, reaching for the lamp to put it out, no doubt. What had there been abnormal or inhuman about the vision, distorted though it must have been in the dim lamplight and shadow? As a man strives to remember the details of a nightmare dream, Steve tried to define in his mind some clear reason that would explain why that flying glimpse had unnerved him to the extent of blundering headlong into a tree, and why the mere vague remembrance of it now caused cold sweat to break out on him.

Cursing himself to keep up his courage, he lighted his lantern, blew out the lamp on the rough table, and resolutely set forth, grasping his pick like a weapon. After all, why should certain seemingly abnormal aspects about a sordid murder upset him? Such crimes were abhorrent, but common enough, especially among Mexicans, who cherished unguessed feuds.

Then as he stepped into the silent starflecked night he brought up short. From across the creek sounded the sudden soul-shaking scream of a horse in deadly terror—then a mad drumming of hoofs that receded in the distance. And Brill swore in rage and dismay. Was it a panther lurking in the hills—had a monster cat slain old Lopez? Then why was not the victim marked with the scars of fierce hooked talons? *And who extinguished the light in the hut?*

140

The Horror From The Mound

As he wondered, Brill was running swiftly toward the dark creek. Not lightly does a cowpuncher regard the stampeding of his stock. As he passed into the darkness of the brush along the dry creek, Brill found his tongue strangely dry. He kept swallowing, and he held the lantern high. It made but faint impression in the gloom, but seemed to accentuate the blackness of the crowding shadows. For some strange reason, the thought entered Brill's chaotic mind that though the land was new to the Anglo-Saxon, it was in reality very old. That broken and desecrated tomb was mute evidence that the land was ancient to man, and suddenly the night and the hills and the shadows bore on Brill with a sense of hideous antiquity. Here had long generations of men lived and died before Brill's ancestors ever heard of the land. In the night, in the shadows of this very creek, men had no doubt given up their ghosts in grisly ways. With these reflections Brill hurried through the shadows of the thick trees.

He breathed deeply in relief when he emerged from the trees on his own side. Hurrying up the gentle slope to the railed corral, he held up his lantern, investigating. The corral was empty; not even the placid cow was in sight. And the bars were down. That pointed to human agency, and the affair took on a newly sinister aspect. Someone did not intend that Brill should ride to Coyote Wells that night. It meant that the murderer intended making his getaway and wanted a good start on the law, or else—Brill grinned wryly. Far away across a mesquite flat he believed he could still catch the faint and faraway noise of running horses. What in God's name had given them such a fright? A cold finger of fear played shudderingly on Brill's spine.

Steve headed for the house. He did not enter boldly. He crept clear around the shack, peering shudderingly into the dark windows, listening with painful intensity for some sound to betray the presence of the lurking killer. At last he ventured to open the door and step in. He threw the door back against the wall to find if anyone were hiding behind it, lifted the lantern high and stepped in, heart pounding, pick gripped fiercely, his feelings a mixture of

The Horror From The Mound

fear and red rage. But no hidden assassin leaped upon him, and a wary exploration of the shack revealed nothing.

With a sigh of relief Brill locked the doors, made fast the windows and lighted his old coal-oil lamp. The thought of old Lopez lying, a glassy-eyed corpse alone in the hut across the creek, made him wince and shiver, but he did not intend to start for town on foot in the night.

He drew from his hiding-place his reliable old Colt .45, spun the blue-steel cylinder, and grinned mirthlessly. Maybe the killer did not intend to leave any witnesses to his crime alive. Well, let him come! He—or they—would find a young cowpuncher with a six-shooter less easy prey than an old unarmed Mexican. And that reminded Brill of the papers he had brought from the hut. Taking care that he was not in line with a window through which a sudden bullet might come, he settled himself to read, with one ear alert for stealthy sounds.

And as he read the crude laborious script, a slow cold horror grew in his soul. It was a tale of fear that the old Mexican had scrawled—a tale handed down from generation—a tale of ancient times.

And Brill read of the wanderings of the caballero Hernando de Estrada and his armored pikemen, who dared the deserts of the Southwest when all was strange and unknown. There were some forty-odd soldiers, servants, and masters, at the beginning, the manuscript ran. There was the captain, de Estrada, and the priest, and young Juan Zavilla, and Don Santiago de Valdez—a mysterious nobleman who had been taken off a helplessly floating ship in the Caribbean Sea—all the others of the crew and passengers had died of plague, he had said, and he had cast their bodies overboard. So de Estrada had taken him aboard the ship that was bearing the expedition from Spain, and de Valdez joined them in their explorations.

Brill read something of their wanderings, told in the crude style of old Lopez, as the old Mexican's ancestors had handed down the tale for over three hundred years. The bare written words dimly reflected the terrific

The Horror From The Mound

hardships the explorers had encountered—drouth, thirst, floods, the desert sandstorms, the spears of hostile red-skins. But it was of another peril that old Lopez told—a grisly lurking horror that fell upon the lonely caravan wandering through the immensity of the wild. Man by man they fell and no man knew the slayer. Fear and black suspicion ate at the heart of the expedition like a canker, and their leader knew not where to turn. This they all knew: among them was a fiend in human form.

Men began to draw apart from each other, to scatter along the line of march, and this mutual suspicion, that sought security in solitude, made it easier for the fiend. The skeleton of the expedition staggered through the wilderness, lost, dazed and helpless, and still the unseen horror hung on their flanks, dragging down the stragglers, preying on drowsing sentries and sleeping men. And on the throat of each was found the wounds of pointed fangs that bled the victim white; so that the living knew with what manner of evil they had to deal. Men reeled through the wild, calling on the saints, or blaspheming in their terror, fighting frenziedly against sleep, until they fell with exhaustion and sleep stole on them with horror and death.

Suspicion centered on a great black man, a cannibal slave from Calabar. And they put him in chains. But young Juan Zavilla went the way of the rest, and then the priest was taken. But the priest fought off his fiendish assailant and lived long enough to gasp the demon's name to de Estrada. And Brill, shuddering and wide-eyed, read:

"... And now it was evident to de Estrada that the good priest had spoken the truth, and the slayer was Don Santiago de Valdez, who was a vampire, an undead fiend, subsisting on the blood of the living. And de Estrada called to mind a certain foul nobleman who had lurked in the mountains of Castile since the days of the Moors, feeding off the blood of helpless victims which lent him a ghastly immortality. This nobleman had been driven forth; none knew where he had fled but it was evident that he and Don Santiago were the same man. He had fled Spain by ship, and de Estrada knew that the people of that

The Horror From The Mound

ship had died, not by plague as the fiend had represented, but by the fangs of the vampire.

"De Estrada and the black man and the few soldiers who still lived went searching for him and found him stretched in bestial sleep in a clump of chaparral; full-gorged he was with human blood from his last victim. Now it is well known that a vampire, like a great serpent, when well gorged, falls into a deep sleep and may be taken without peril. But de Estrada was at a loss as to how to dispose of the monster, for how may the dead be slain? For a vampire is a man who has died long ago, yet is quick with a certain foul unlife.

"The men urged that the Caballero drive a stake through the fiend's heart and cut off his head, uttering the holy words that would crumble the long-dead body into dust, but the priest was dead and de Estrada feared that in the act the monster might waken.

"So they took Don Santiago, lifting him softly, and bore him to an old Indian mound near by. This they opened, taking forth the bones they found there, and they placed the vampire within and sealed up the mound—*Dios* grant until Judgment Day.

"It is a place accursed, and I wish I had starved elsewhere before I came into this part of the country seeking work—for I have known of the land and the creek and the mound with its terrible secret, ever since childhood; so you see, Senor Brill, why you must not open the mound and wake the fiend—"

There the manuscript ended with an erratic scratch of the pencil that tore the crumpled leaf.

Brill rose, his heart pounding wildly, his face bloodless, his tongue cleaving to his palate. He gagged and found words.

"That's why the spur was in the mound—one of them Spaniards dropped it while they was diggin'—and I mighta knowed it's been dug into before, the way the charcoal was scattered out—but, good God—"

Aghast he shrank from the black visions—an undead monster stirring in the gloom of his tomb,

144

The Horror From The Mound

thrusting from within to push aside the stone loosened by the pick of ignorance—a shadowy shape loping over the hill toward a light that betokened a human prey—a frightful long arm that crossed a dim-lighted window....

"It's madness!" he gasped. "Lopez was plumb loco! They ain't no such things as vampires! If they is, why didn't he get me first, instead of Lopez—unless he was scoutin' around, makin' sure of everything before he pounced? Aw, hell! It's all a pipe-dream—"

The words froze in his throat. At the window a face glared and gibbered soundlessly at him. Two icy eyes pierced his very soul. A shriek burst from his throat and that ghastly visage vanished. But the very air was permeated by the foul scent that had hung about the ancient mound. And now the door creaked—bent slowly inward. Brill backed up against the wall, his gun shaking in his hand. It did not occur to him to fire through the door; in his chaotic brain he had but one thought—that only that thin portal of wood separated him from some horror born out of the womb of night and gloom and the black past. His eyes were distended as he saw the door give, as he heard the staples of the bolt groan.

The door burst inward. Brill did not scream. His tongue was frozen to the roof of his mouth. His fear-glazed eyes took in the tall, vulture-like form—the icy eyes, the long black finger nails—the moldering garb, hideously ancient—the long spurred boot—the slouch hat with its crumbling feather—the flowing cloak that was falling to slow shreds. Framed in the black doorway crouched that abhorrent shape out of the past, and Brill's brain reeled. A savage cold radiated from the figure—the scent of moldering clay and charnel-house refuse. And then the undead came at the living like a swooping vulture.

Brill fired point-blank and saw a shred of rotten cloth fly from the Thing's breast. The vampire reeled beneath the impact of the heavy ball, then righted himself and came on with frightful speed. Brill reeled back against the wall with a choking cry, the gun falling from his

The Horror From The Mound

nerveless hand. The black legends were true then—human weapons were powerless—for may a man kill one already dead for long centuries, as mortals die?

Then the clawlike hands at his throat roused the young cowpuncher to a frenzy of madness. As his pioneer ancestors fought hand to hand against brain-shattering odds, Steve Brill fought the cold dead crawling thing that sought his life and his soul.

Of that ghastly battle Brill never remembered much. It was a blind chaos in which he screamed beast-like, tore and slugged and hammered, where long black nails like the talons of a panther tore at him, and pointed teeth snapped again and again at his throat. Rolling and tumbling about the room, both half enveloped by the musty folds of that ancient rotting cloak, they smote and tore at each other among the ruins of the shattered furniture, and the fury of the vampire was not more terrible than the fear-crazed desperation of his victim.

They crashed headlong into the table, knocking it down upon its side, and the coal oil lamp splintered on the floor, spraying the walls with sudden flames. Brill felt the bite of the burning oil that splattered him, but in the red frenzy of the fight he gave no heed. The black talons were tearing at him, the inhuman eyes burning icily into his soul; between his frantic fingers the withered flesh of the monster was hard as dry wood. And wave after wave of blind madness swept over Steve Brill. Like a man battling a nightmare he screamed and smote, while all about them the fire leaped up and caught at the walls and roof.

Through darting jets and licking tongues of flames they reeled and rolled like a demon and a mortal warring on the fire-lanced floors of hell. And in the growing tumult of the flames, Brill gathered himself for one last volcanic burst of frenzied strength. Breaking away and staggering up, gasping and bloody, he lunged blindly at the foul shape and caught it in a grip not even the vampire could break. And whirling his fiendish assailant bodily on high, he dashed him down across the uptilted edge of the fallen table as a man might break a stick of wood across his knee. Something cracked like a snapping branch and the vampire fell from Brill's grasp to writhe in a strange broken posture on the burning floor. Yet it was not dead, for its flaming eyes still burned on Brill with a ghastly hunger, and it strove to crawl toward him with its broken spine, as a dying snake crawls.

Brill, reeling and gasping, shook the blood from his eyes, and staggered blindly through the broken door. And as a man runs from the portals of hell, he ran stumblingly through the mesquite and chaparral until he fell from utter exhaustion. Looking back he saw the flames of the burning house and thanked God that it would burn until the very bones of Don Santiago de Valdez were utterly consumed and destroyed from the knowledge of men.

ABOUT THE AUTHOR

ROBERT ERVIN HOWARD was born in the small town of Cross Plains, Texas, in 1906. His first story, "Spear and Fang," was published when he was eighteen, in *Weird Tales*. Over the next twelve years, Howard wrote over a million words of fantasy, Westerns, pirate yarns, detective and adventure stories for the pulp magazines. He is best known for his larger-than-life heroes: King Kull, Solomon Kane, Bran Mak Morn, and the greatest hero of them all, Conan, who swagger through exotic and far-off lands and times having fabulous adventures, conquering kingdoms and beautiful women with equal ease. Howard committed suicide on June 11, 1936, when he heard his mother had lapsed into a terminal coma.

OUT OF THIS WORLD!

That's the only way to describe Bantam's great series of science fiction classics. These space-age thrillers are filled with terror, fancy and adventure and written by America's most renowned writers of science fiction. Welcome to outer space and have a good trip!

☐ 11392	**STAR TREK: THE NEW VOYAGES 2** by Culbreath & Marshak	$1.95
☐ 13179	**THE MARTIAN CHRONICLES** by Ray Bradbury	$2.25
☐ 12588	**SOMETHING WICKED THIS WAY COMES** by Ray Bradbury	$1.95
☐ 12753	**STAR TREK: THE NEW VOYAGES** by Culbreath & Marshak	$1.95
☐ 13260	**ALAS BABYLON** by Pat Frank	$2.25
☐ 13006	**A CANTICLE FOR LEIBOWITZ** by Walter Miller, Jr.	$2.25
☐ 12673	**HELLSTROM'S HIVE** by Frank Herbert	$1.95
☐ 12454	**DEMON SEED** by Dean R. Koontz	$1.95
☐ 11662	**SONG OF THE PEARL** by Ruth Nichols	$1.75
☐ 11599	**THE FARTHEST SHORE** by Ursula LeGuin	$1.95
☐ 11600	**THE TOMBS OF ATUAN** by Ursula LeGuin	$1.95
☐ 11609	**A WIZARD OF EARTHSEA** by Ursula LeGuin	$1.95
☐ 12005	**20,000 LEAGUES UNDER THE SEA** by Jules Verne	$1.50
☐ 11417	**STAR TREK XI** by James Blish	$1.50
☐ 12655	**FANTASTIC VOYAGE** by Isaac Asimov	$1.95
☐ 12477	**NEBULA AWARD STORIES ELEVEN** Ursula LeGuin, ed.	$1.95

Buy them at your local bookstore or use this handy coupon for ordering:

Bantam Books, Inc., Dept. SF, 414 East Golf Road, Des Plaines, Ill. 60016

Please send me the books I have checked above. I am enclosing $_____ (please add 75¢ to cover postage and handling). Send check or money order —no cash or C.O.D.'s please.

Mr/Mrs/Miss_____

Address_____

City_____State/Zip_____

SF—9/79

Please allow four weeks for delivery. This offer expires 3/80.

FANTASY AND SCIENCE FICTION FAVORITES

Bantam brings you the recognized classics as well as the current favorites in fantasy and science fantasy. Here you will find the beloved Conan books along with recent titles by the most respected authors in the genre.

☐	12757	NOVA Samuel R. Delany	$1.95
☐	12680	TRITON Samuel R. Delany	$2.25
☐	12881	DHALGREN Samuel R. Delany	$2.50
☐	11950	ROGUE IN SPACE Frederic Brown	$1.75
☐	12018	CONAN THE SWORDSMAN #1 DeCamp & Carter	$1.95
☐	12706	CONAN THE LIBERATOR #2 DeCamp & Carter	$1.95
☐	12031	SKULLS IN THE STARS: Solomon Kane #1 Robert E. Howard	$1.95
☐	11139	THE MICRONAUTS Gordon Williams	$1.95
☐	11276	THE GOLDEN SWORD Janet Morris	$1.95
☐	11835	DRAGONSINGER Anne McCaffrey	$1.95
☐	13360	DRAGONSONG Anne McCaffrey	$2.25
☐	10879	JONAH KIT Ian Watson	$1.50
☐	12019	KULL Robert E. Howard	$1.95
☐	10779	MAN PLUS Frederik Pohl	$1.95
☐	12269	TIME STORM Gordon R. Dickson	$2.25

Buy them at your local bookstore or use this handy coupon for ordering:

Bantam Books, Inc., Dept. SF2, 414 East Golf Road, Des Plaines, Ill. 60016

Please send me the books I have checked above. I am enclosing $_____ (please add 75¢ to cover postage and handling). Send check or money order —no cash or C.O.D.'s please.

Mr/Mrs/Miss _____

Address _____

City _____ State/Zip _____

SF2—9/79

Please allow four weeks for delivery. This offer expires 3/80.

Bantam Book Catalog

Here's your up-to-the-minute listing of over 1,400 titles by your favorite authors.

This illustrated, large format catalog gives a description of each title. For your convenience, it is divided into categories in fiction and non-fiction—gothics, science fiction, westerns, mysteries, cookbooks, mysticism and occult, biographies, history, family living, health, psychology, art.

So don't delay—take advantage of this special opportunity to increase your reading pleasure.

Just send us your name and address and 50¢ (to help defray postage and handling costs).

BANTAM BOOKS, INC.
Dept. FC, 414 East Golf Road, Des Plaines, Ill. 60016

Mr./Mrs./Miss_____
(please print)

Address_____

City_____ State_____ Zip_____

Do you know someone who enjoys books? Just give us their names and addresses and we'll send them a catalog too!

Mr./Mrs./Miss_____
Address_____
City_____ State_____ Zip_____

Mr./Mrs./Miss_____
Address_____
City_____ State_____ Zip_____

FC—9/76